Valentine's Blizzard Murder

Linnea West

Valentine's Blizzard Murder

•Chapter One•

The end credits rolled on the romantic comedy on the television and suddenly I could hear the wind screeching by outside the window. When the weather guy said a winter storm was coming, I guess he hadn't been kidding. I grabbed the remote from the side table and flipped to the local station where a large, red warning box was scrolling across the bottom of a sitcom rerun.

BLIZZARD WARNING

I glanced over at Clark, who was sitting on the other end of the couch and at Mandy, who was in the arm chair. They both looked a bit worried and I couldn't really blame them. Minnesotans take a winter storm warning with both a healthy dose of skepticism and a feeling of unnecessary preparation. Once the weather report this morning had firmed up the idea that a winter storm was actually coming and had been upgraded to a blizzard, my father had run out to stock up on candles, some bottles of water, batteries, and a few other necessities. Not everyone does that, I'm sure. But not everyone runs a bed and

3

breakfast and wants their guests to have a pleasant experience no matter what Mother Nature has in store for them.

My parents had five children and were living in a large, beautiful, old Victorian house. When most of us moved out, they didn't want to let go of the place. They were already familiar with the hospitality industry because they also own a motel in Shady Lake. So instead of selling, they renovated the house and opened up the Shady Lake Bed & Breakfast. And by a cruel twist of fate, I am living with them once again at the age of thirty.

I left Shady Lake after high school and thought I'd never look back. I went to college and then moved to the Twin Cities with my husband Peter. I was working an office job in marketing and living it up at clubs, brunch, and fancy exercise classes.

And then my entire world crumbled down around me when Peter died in a car accident one morning on his way to work. It was like everything stopped. My job became meaningless. I couldn't sleep because the apartment just seemed so big and empty once I was alone. All of a sudden, I was scared of the dark.

Once my parents understood the full

spectrum of how I was doing, they jumped into action and drove up to get me. When they appeared on my doorstep that morning, I had been sitting up in a chair most of the night with a flashlight in hand trying to to simultaneously get some sleep and stay up in case the darkness tried to close in on me.

Now almost a year later, I'm here in the living room with Clark Hutchins, one of the men I've been casually seeing, and Mandy, my best friend. And I'm slowly healing. I'm not going to live with my parents forever, but right now it is my safe place to land.

When the house was turned into a B&B, my parents built an addition on the back over a garage where they could live with Tank, my youngest brother who is still in high school. In the great state of Minnesota, owners must live on site in their bed and breakfast. The only problem was that they thought they'd be empty nesters once Tank moved on in another year. Instead, I moved in and took over the library they built in the addition.

"Tessa, I should probably try to get Mandy home," Clark said, taking my hand. "It sounds nasty out there."

Listening to the wind, I knew he was

right but feeling his hand holding mine, I didn't want him to. Clark frequently took my breath away. He was a hot commodity in Shady Lake because he only moved here a few years ago to teach at the high school. He was literally tall, dark, and handsome and I kept wondering what he saw in me. No matter what, I was having fun going out with him.

"You don't have to drive me," Mandy said. "I'll just stay here and go home tomorrow."

Mandy is my best friend and she looks a lot like me, but only the me that is living my best life. She owned the Donut Hut and while that was the leading cause for my rapidly expanding waistline, she somehow managed to not overindulge. In fact, she managed not to indulge hardly at all. But while she is the supplier of most of my sweets, she is also the one who has a salad every day for lunch and encourages me to do the same.

We have been best friends for a very long time. In high school, Mandy and I would hang out just the two of us a lot; we didn't really have other friends. Mandy became more like a sister than a friend. After high school, though, we walked totally different paths. I left Shady Lake, but Mandy stayed. She took over the Donut Hut from her parents, who retired to Florida. She even moved into the apartment above the Donut Hut and she lives there now with her long time boyfriend, Trevor.

"Of course you can stay, Mandy," I said. "But let's go downstairs and actually get a look at what the weather is like outside."

Clark stood up and stretched his arms over his head before offering me his hands. I put my small hands in his large, warm hands and he pulled me up off of the couch. I lingered in the moment, not wanting to let him go. His dark eyes sparkled as he searched my face and a big smile spread across Clark's face.

After a moment, I ripped myself away from his gaze and went to grab Clark's jacket from the little coat rack. He slipped his arms into the sleeves and we headed out into the B&B and down the stairs. The instant we emerged in the front entry hall, it was clear that the blizzard was here.

Even though it was only mid-afternoon, it was so dark that it looked like it was the middle of the night. Outside, we couldn't even see down the driveway because it was blowing snow so hard. The tree branches were whipping around so hard that I was surprised they weren't just ripping right off of the trees. I glanced at Clark's face and I could see that he really didn't want to go outside. I can't say I blame him.

"You aren't going to try to drive home, right Clark?"

My dad strolled in from the living room where he had been watching the storm out of the large picture window. My dad is an avid bird watcher, so much that the B&B is bird themed with each guest room being named after a bird common to Minnesota. Normally, he watches the bird feeders outside the window but tonight they were swinging violently in the wind.

"Hello Mr. Schmidt," Clark said. "I was just about to head out before the storm gets worse."

"No you won't," my dad said. "You can stay here tonight. There's a pull-out sofa in Tank's room."

Tank was lucky enough to stay in what was going to be a guest room once he graduated high school. It was a large suite with an attached bathroom and even a little living room space. I tried not to be jealous since my bedroom was so small I could almost touch both walls when I stood in the middle of the room. But I also knew that no one had planned on me living here and hopefully I wouldn't be here for long.

Clark hesitated and I could see some emotions dancing across his face. He was trying to decide whether to try to be the macho guy who stands by his decision or to be the grateful guy who didn't want to go out in the storm. After wrestling silently with his thoughts for a moment, he gave a curt nod.

"Thank you Mr. Schmidt," he said. "I'll gladly take you up on that offer."

"Why don't you go up and help Tank get the couch set up," my dad said. "I'm going to put these girls to work setting up some extra chairs at the dinner table for tonight."

Clark grabbed my hand and gave it a quick squeeze before he hung his jacket up in the entry way and bounded up the stairs, back towards the family section of the B&B.

"We are full up girls," my dad said once Clark was out of sight. "Between Valentine's Day being this weekend and Jake Crawford staying here, all of the rooms are full and everyone will be stuck here for dinner plus a few extras, like Mandy and Clark."

I had almost forgotten about Jake Crawford. He was originally from Shady

Lake and was here for a few days on his honeymoon. He was also a minor celebrity, but in a small town like this, any bit of celebrity is cause for a huge celebration. Jake had moved to California after high school and since then, he had starred in a few huge commercials and even had a minor role on a popular sitcom. His parents still lived here with his grandparents so when Jake got married and his grandparents weren't able to travel to the wedding, Jake set up a trip back to Shady Lake as part of his honeymoon.

Unfortunately, that meant he brought his wife Anna with him. After they had checked in, I had tried my hardest to steer clear of her because she was not from a small town. As a lifelong, big city, California girl, Anna had not been happy to come to Nowheresville Minnesota as part of her honeymoon. She and Jake visited his parents and grandparents a few times and Jake had taken her on a small tour of Shady Lake, but judging from her face when she came back ten minutes later, it had not gone well. Anna spent most of her time since on her laptop or smart phone. I'm not exactly sure what she is doing all of the time, but she seems to be scrolling and clicking away like she knows what she is doing.

I looked behind my dad into the living room and saw that the room was otherwise empty. Anna must be up in her room. Or maybe, if we were lucky, she was stuck out somewhere in the storm and wouldn't be able to make it back. Hopefully she would be stuck somewhere with Jake because he wasn't really what you would call a pleasant person either.

Whenever Jake came back to Shady Lake, he was the definition of "big fish in a small pond." He expected everyone to bend over backward to accommodate him. After all, didn't we know he was a big star? Didn't we all see him every Tuesday night on the television? Wasn't he gracious to come back and visit all of us lowly Shady Lakers? From what I gather, it had been bad enough to simply encounter him around town. Now that I was back and had to deal with him at the B&B, he was almost unbearable.

I snapped back to attention, realizing my inner rage was making me zone out. My dad was still droning on about dinner and how we would accommodate everyone and Mandy stood politely listening, nodding her head every once in a while to show how interested she was pretending to be.

"Okay Dad," I said. "Mandy and I really should get those arrangements going."

I grabbed her sleeve and gave her a tug towards the dining room before my dad could ramble on any more.

•Chapter Two•

The dining room was one of my favorite rooms in the B&B. Down the middle of the room was a giant, Craftsman style dining table. It was beautiful and it was polished regularly to maintain a beautiful shine. It was surrounded by twelve matching chairs and I was almost a little bit sad that we would have to squeeze some ugly folding chairs around it too.

But as beautiful as the table was, my favorite thing about this room was that it was always decorated seasonally. When I moved back in, I took over decorating this room specifically because it brought me such joy. I loved anything that had to do with holidays, any holiday really. Taking over the seasonal decorating was my favorite part of working at the B&B.

As Valentine's Day was so near, the dining room was currently decked out in hearts and red and pink. One wall had a giant china cabinet and inside I had interspersed little wooden hearts painted red and pink. On the other wall, above a buffet table that was stained to match the dining table, I had hung up a banner of red and pink felt hearts. On the buffet table was a bouquet of roses and a small sign that declared *Happy Valentine's Day*.

The challenge to decorating the room was to do it in a way that was understated and elegant because if you put one too many hearts in there all of a sudden the vibe changes from a classy bed and breakfast to that of an elementary school Valentine's Day party. Whenever I opened up the double doors that lead into the dining room, I was pleased to see just how good it looked.

And now we were going to spoil it with some old, gray folding chairs that my parents had bought from Shady Lake Lutheran Church one year when the church bought new tables for the Gathering Room and got rid of all of the old ones. They were sturdy chairs and were actually quite comfortable, as far as folding chairs go. But they were ugly as sin and would totally clash with my beautiful decorations.

I let out a big sigh and turned to Mandy, who was busy chomping on a piece of gum while she inspected the decorations. Miss Good Healthy Habits had one gross, decades-long habit that she couldn't quite get over. Mandy was a gum chewer. No, not a gum chewer. She should be called a gum chomper. She was forever chewing her gum so loudly that I can't hear myself think. I've given up trying to tell her to stop because it does no good. She just can't quit gum.

"I'll go get the chairs if you start trying to figure out where they all will go," I said. Mandy nodded and I left her to her chomping while I ran down to the basement. The door to the basement was by the back door in the kitchen, so I pushed through the swinging door to the kitchen where I almost walked straight into Dawn Wilder, another guest in the bed and breakfast.

"I just wanted to lend a hand," Dawn was saying as I came in. "I love cooking at home and I just thought I could help out here."

My dad had a forced smile on his face. Typically, my father was a cheerful guy, but when he was in the kitchen, he just wanted everyone to get out of his way. At least he was a bit more polite than when I got in his way.

"That is very nice of you Dawn," my dad said through clenched teeth. "But part of my job is to cook for the guests and the guests are supposed to eat and enjoy what I cook. You are a guest, so you can just go out there and enjoy the dinner, as soon as it is done."

Dawn's bottom lip pushed out until it protruded out past her chin. She shook her head, which made her dark brown braid bounce all around her shoulders. After a moment, her face shifted into annoyance, her eyebrows knitting together and her mouth set in a firm line.

"Isn't part of your job also to make me happy as a guest?" she demanded. "What would make me happy is to help you cook."

My dad turned slowly to look at Dawn and my mouth dropped open. That was some crazy audacity coming out of this woman. She was tiny, only coming up to my shoulder but she was full of fire. Was she just so bored that she needed something to do?

I looked at my dad's face just as his eyes shifted to me. The confusion in his eyes floated towards me and I decided to take my turn to discourage her before my dad ran her out of the kitchen by force.

"Miss Wilder, I could show you our selection of board games otherwise we have a bookshelf of books in the living room that are free for the taking," I said, shifting into my customer service voice.

"Hello there Tessa," Dawn said.

Something inside of her seemed to shift once she realized that there was someone else here to force her out of the kitchen. "That is a sweet offer. I suppose I will go take a look at the bookshelf. Thank you for the suggestion."

She stood and stared at us for a moment before she turned and left the kitchen. The door swinging back and forth behind her a few times before it finally shut. I turned and looked at my father, who was already back at the stove stirring the multiple pots that were simmering.

"That was weird," I said as I walked towards the stove. "What's for dinner Dad?"

"Oh I'm just cooking up some pad thai," my dad said casually, like that was something he always made. Actually, I was kind of assuming he had never made this before, but I wasn't going to ask because when my dad was in the kitchen cooking, you don't ask questions. "Thank you, by the way. That woman just would not leave and I didn't know how to nicely get her to leave."

I laughed as I took in the delicious smells that were wafting off of the stove. Somehow my father was making pad thai that was at least as good if not better than any I'd ever had before. I guess I hadn't tasted it yet, but I was sure that it would be amazing. My dad had this ability to just decide to make something and then totally nail it on the first attempt. He was just lucky, I guess.

"I'm going to head down to the basement to get the chairs, okay?" I said as I gave him a one-arm hug around his shoulders. He briefly tapped his head down onto mine, which was as much of a hug as I was going to get while he was cooking.

Just past the eating nook in the kitchen was a door leading down to the basement. When I was younger, I hated going down there. The staircase isn't so bad. There is a light switch at the top that lights a single bulb hanging over the stairs that lit them up quite nicely.

But once you get to the bottom, it is a different story. The basement is just a series of dank, dark, concrete rooms and the lights were sparse. Every few yards, there was a light hanging from the ceiling that would only turn on with a pull chain. When I was really young, I couldn't reach the pull chains so I avoided coming down here as much as I could.

And then I made the mistake of watching a scary movie as a teenager where there was a scene of the killer running up a set of stairs and for some reason, my mind linked that to the basement stairs. So even once I was big enough to pull the chains, I avoided the basement because my mind just flashed back to that movie.

Now, I had been able to set aside the scary movie, but losing Peter had brought about an inexplicable fear of the dark. I had big, heavy-duty flashlights stashed anywhere I might need them. One weighs down my purse, another is taking up most of the glove compartment of my station wagon, and another is here, at the top of the basement staircase on a shelf along with a hammer, a jar of nails, and some other things that were routinely needed around the B&B.

I grabbed the dark red, metal flashlight and flicked it on, even though the stairs were already lit up by the overhead light. The stairs were older and no matter how many times I'd used them, I always took them carefully. As I went down, the air around me turned frigid. Even though the furnace is downstairs, all of the heat was sucked upstairs which left the basement freezing cold.

Once I was at the bottom, I pointed my

flashlight towards the next light bulb. First, I flashed the light around the room and just took in the surroundings before I dashed to the light bulb and yanked on the little metal chain that dangled above my head. It sprung to life and lit up the first room. I felt a bit foolish, but no one else was down here to watch me dash from light to light.

Thankfully, the folding chairs were here in the first room and I wouldn't have to deal with the other rooms. The only problem was that I wouldn't be able to carry the chairs and the flashlight back up the stairs. Oh well, I would just have to come back down to shut off the light bulb and get the flashlight. I hefted two folding chairs up into each arm and headed back towards the stairs.

As I climbed carefully back up to the main level, the cold of the metal chairs was seeping through the sleeves of my shirt. I hoped they would be able to warm up a bit before everyone sits down to dinner otherwise four people were going to have very cold bottoms.

Once I was back up into the kitchen, I was surprised to see that my father was gone, but a different guest was loitering around the bowls of pad thai that my father had started ladling out.

"Excuse me sir," I said as politely as possible. "But guests aren't allowed in the kitchen."

The man spun to face me, obviously completely unaware that I had made my appearance from some mysterious door at the back of the kitchen. It was Lyle Roberts, who was here for the Valentine's Day weekend with his wife Claudia. He was the sort of man who had probably always been handsome and he had managed to make his aging look graceful. His jet black hair had just a few flecks of gray that made him look distinguished.

"Oh, hello there," Lyle said. He quickly masked his surprise by leaning casually on the counter next to the bowls of pad thai. "I just came in to check and see if dinner was almost ready, but there was no one here."

"So you just decided to hang out with the food?" I said.

Before either of us could speak again, the swinging door to the kitchen opened up and my father came back in, followed closely by Anna Crawford, who was somehow managing to walk while scrolling on her phone. My dad stopped and his eyebrows knit together in surprise.

"Oh hello, Lyle, Tessa," he said with a nod of his head. "I just stepped out to find someone to help me set the table and I found Anna in the living room. Things are a bit different today since we are all stuck here because of the blizzard."

As my dad said the last part, he gave me a little tip of the head which probably was meant to tell me to calm myself and relax the rules a little bit. I shrugged at him and continued to schlep the chairs through the kitchen towards the dining room.

"Come on Lyle and Anna," my father said. "Each of you grab two bowls and lets get them on the table. Everything else is set and there are name tags at each spot."

My father followed me through the door with a few bowls of food with Anna close behind and Lyle a little further back. The dining room was already somewhat full with Mandy, my mother, and a few of the other guests drifting in to have dinner. My father and Anna plopped the bowls down on the table while Lyle appeared to be reading the name tags before remembering that he was supposed to be delivering food.

After a few more trips to bring bowls back and forth, the table was set and dinner was served.

"Everyone find your spot," my father said. "Time for dinner."

●Chapter Three●

For a while, the only sounds were the clinking of silverware and a muttered compliment to the chef here and there. I wasn't sure if everything felt strange just because here we were in a bed and breakfast having dinner together, but there was some sort of tension floating through the air.

I looked around the table at the guests, realizing what a ragtag bunch we were. The bed and breakfast usually hosted a gaggle of older couples in town to visit grandchildren. Every once in a while a local young couple would take a honeymoon night here. But this week was very different.

Jake Crawford and his wife Anna were here. I had to admit that Jake was handsome and I could definitely understand why he had landed work as an actor. Anna was a California girl through and through, with long, waist length blond hair. Jake was currently frowning at his pad thai, taking a drink of his wine instead. I tried not to stare at him, but you know how sometimes there is someone who is just so pretty that you can't look away? That's Jake.

I shoved another bite of pad thai in my mouth and looked back just in time to see Jake pat his wife's hand before scowling at Lyle, who was sitting across from him. I assumed Lyle may have kicked him by accident. The one thing about this table is that it is somewhat narrow, so kicking your across-the-table neighbor happens too often.

Lyle and his wife Claudia were across the table. Where Lyle was strikingly handsome for a middle aged man, Claudia was very plain. She was the sort of person who was completely forgettable. Her clothes tonight looked just like what she had worn everyday since they arrived here. She was wearing a gray v-neck t-shirt and a pair of jeans with a simple cardigan sweater. If Claudia had jazzed it up with a necklace or a scarf, she could have looked very fashionable. But instead, she sort of faded into the background.

Like I should be one to talk, I am definitely not a fashion plate. I looked down at myself, realizing I was only slightly dressed up because Clark was over. I had a pair of skinny jeans on and I had pulled on a white, long sleeved tee and a maroon colored cocoon sweater. To jazz it up a little, I had a long black pendant necklace and a few sparkly bobby pins holding back a few pieces of hair. Mandy was the one I should really thank for helping me out with my fashion. When I was living in the big city, working my desk job, I depended on an online wardrobe subscription box to dress me. Now that I was back in Shady Lake, Mandy was the one who would help me put outfits together.

Right now, Mandy was sitting next to me and my mother at the end of the table. We were each squished onto the corners of the table while my mother was in the middle. I tried to give the guests their space while squishing the people who lived here or were stuck here at the ends. That meant at the head of the table, Clark and Tank were squashed onto the corners while my father kept his head of the table spot.

There were two other older couples who were here to celebrate, Linda and her husband Dave and Cheryl and her husband Joe. The two couples were best friends and actually lived in Shady Lake, but Linda and Cheryl had decided that staying at the Shady Lake Bed and Breakfast would be a special way to celebrate Valentine's Day and their husbands had grudgingly come along.

The two guests who were somewhat out of place were Chelsea and Dawn. We didn't get a lot of single guests here as bed and breakfasts tended to draw out more couples than anything else, but every once in a while we would have one. The strange thing was that we had two this week, although Chelsea was only here as a journalist to follow Jake's visit back to town.

As I looked down the table, Chelsea sneered at me from above her bowl. Chelsea and I had been in school together and for some unknown reason, she hated me. I can't say that I enjoy her company either as every time I'm around her, all she does is glare at me and snip at me. Of course, I wish I could say I was the bigger person who rose above it, but I typically lowered myself down to her level and threw insults right back.

Chelsea worked for the local newspaper and she was usually stuck writing obituaries and little pieces like who bowled 300 that week or who won the big prize at bingo. Every once in a while, though, she was given a chance at a big story and I wondered how much she had to beg to get this assignment. No matter what, she was dedicated to writing a good story because she had paid for her room herself. I know because I sneaked a peek at the register.

The other woman who was here by herself was Dawn. She had light brown hair that was braided in a french braid down the middle of her head. Dawn's style seemed to be very casual. She was currently wearing a pair of dark purple joggers and thin, black hoodie shirt. She looked like she was about to pop out to a workout class. I didn't know much about her because she had kept to herself. As I took another bite of dinner, I watched Dawn as she tried to sneakily stare at Jake. I couldn't blame her, of course, as I had been doing the same thing earlier. I took a glance at her hand and noticed that she wasn't wearing a wedding ring. So I guess I knew one thing about her.

"Well then, maybe we should all go around and say something about ourselves like a fun fact since we are all stuck here for a while," Linda said with a clap of her hands.

Cheryl nodded enthusiastically along with her friend as both of their husbands rolled their eyes knowingly at each other. I got the sense that this was a running theme in their relationship and honestly, it just made me want to be their friend also.

"I'll go first," Linda said. "My name is

Linda and I have an odd hobby of making lamps. Like sometimes I will revamp lamps I find at second hand shops and sometimes I make weird things into lamps, like a log shaped like a shark that I bought from a guy at the fair who carves them with a chainsaw."

Linda picked up her wine glass and triumphantly took a drink before motioning towards her husband Dave, who was sitting quietly together.

"My name is Dave," he said, obviously used to going along with his wife's schemes. "And my house is full of lamps."

I just about spit out the sip of wine I had just taken and as the table burst into laughter, Linda playfully smacked him on the arm. Dave's friend Joe was guffawing so much that he went into a coughing fit, which seemed to just make everyone laugh even more.

"Okay Jake, you are next," Linda said, leaning across Dave to put her hand on Jake's arm.

Jake was staring at his bowl with his eyebrows furrowed. He was slowly chewing a bite of his pad thai. Looking at his bowl, he had only had a few bites of the very full bowl. He swallowed what was in his mouth and turned towards my father, ignoring Linda's gentle prodding to take his turn at the game.

"Mr. Schmidt, is there fish sauce in this?" he asked.

"No, of course not," my dad said, his face going pale. "Why, what's wrong?"

"I'm just feeling a little funny," Jake said. "I think I'm going to go to my room."

He pushed his chair back and stood up, but suddenly clutched at his throat and sank down to the floor. Jake's eyes bulged out and his face started to turn red. Everyone turned to look as it slowly dawned on the room that something was terribly wrong.

•Chapter Four•

I have a theory that there are two kinds of people: those that are good in an emergency and those that aren't. This was one of those times where the world sorted themselves neatly out into those two categories. While Dave, Clark, Mandy, Dawn, Tank, and I all rushed over to help, everyone else just sat in their chairs, staring and processing what was happening.

"Jake, are you okay?" Anna cried, shoving her chair back as she realized that something was wrong. "I think he's having an allergic reaction. He's got a severe fish allergy."

"Does he have one of those needle things with medicine?" Dave asked. For someone who had just made the room laugh, he had transformed into problem solver quickly enough. I could see his mind racing as he tried to make a plan of attack. I don't think he had been a doctor, but he must have been someone who needed to take charge in situations.

Anna turned slowly, as if she were in a dream. She looked at him for a moment before nodding and dashing out of the room. Anna ran almost as if she were running tentatively through a fog. She almost ran into the door frame as she left the dining room. Clark started after her, pausing for a minute at the foot of the table.

"Don't worry Tessa, I'll help her out," Clark said before he ran out of the room after her, much more sure-footed than Anna.

I bent down next to Jake, not sure what to do to help him. I didn't know much about food allergies or if there was anything I could do to help. Jake stared helplessly up at me as his face started to swell up. I felt someone kneel next to me and looking over, I saw Claudia taking one of his hands. There were tears in her eyes as she squeezed his hand.

"But there isn't any fish in the pad thai," my dad cried. He was still sitting at the head of the table, his fork halfway to his mouth. His face was screwed up in confusion and after a moment, he realized he should probably do something. He stood up and after a look around the room, he started to clear the dishes. I was about to stop him, but I figured that if he had some sort of task, it was better than nothing.

"Is there any other allergy medicine we

could try?" Mandy asked. Her face was solemn and serious. She was on autopilot emergency response right now.

I wasn't sure that would do anything as Jake's breathing was labored and I could tell from the sound that his throat was swelling shut. That meant that the chance of any medicine going down was slim to none, but we had to do something. Where was Anna with the lifesaving medicine? She obviously realized that this was an emergency situation, so why was it taking her so long?

"There is some allergy medicine in the kitchen cabinet," my mother said, lazily pointing towards the kitchen. She looked like she was in some sort of dream.

Mandy and Tank looked at each other and raced through the swinging door into the kitchen where I could hear them slamming cabinet doors open and shut as they searched in vain.

As my father came to grab more dishes, I grabbed his pants leg and jerked on it a few times until he finally realized what I was doing and looked down at me.

"Do not clear Jake's plate," I said quietly, hoping no one else could hear me. The only other person who was close to me was Dawn. "We need to check it to see if there is anything different about it."

My dad blinked at me a few times before moving on. He was drifting around in a daze, collecting dishes. I sometimes wondered how he and my mother got through all of our childhood accidents if neither of them did well in an accident. I suppose that is why I was the one that often took charge. Someone had to.

Jake slumped down more and Dawn laid his head in her lap as I raced through the first aid training I did back in high school, but nothing was coming to mind. The only thing I knew about an allergic reaction was to use one of those medicine pens to stop anaphylaxis. But where was the medicine? If Jake had this bad of an allergy, he should have it somewhere easily accessible. Why was it taking Anna and Clark so long to find it?

Mandy came bursting out of the kitchen with Tank hot on her heels. She was waving a bottle of liquid allergy medicine and a measuring spoon. She practically threw the spoon at me as she twisted the childproof cap off with no trouble at all.

I held the spoon as she carefully poured it out, filling the spoon with the sickly, pink liquid. We weren't really trying to measure.

At this point, what would a little extra allergy medicine do to Jake? Once it was full, I held it up to Jake's lips and tried to tip it in. His eyes were wildly dashing around the room as the liquid spilled out of his mouth and all over his shirt instead of going down his throat.

"It's no use," I said. "His throat is swollen so much that the medicine won't go down. I think we should keep trying though."

Dawn started to cry as Mandy poured another spoonful of medicine for me. I tried to force it into Jake's mouth but once again the medicine came spilling out, making a large, sticky spot on the collar of Jake's shirt.

Jake's beautiful blue eyes were now rolling into the back of his head. I grabbed his wrist and felt all over for his pulse, finally feeling a very faint heartbeat. Jake's pulse was rapidly slowing down and his breathing was becoming even more labored.

I could tell I was losing him and I wasn't sure what to do about it. I realized suddenly that we hadn't even called the emergency number, although I wasn't sure they would be able to get to us anyway because of the weather.

"Tank, I need you to call for an

ambulance," I said. We locked eyes, both knowing that even if the ambulance could make it through the storm, they might not make it in time. He pushed through the swinging door into the kitchen, but a moment later he stepped back out with the corded phone in his hand.

"The phone lines must be down," Tank said. "There isn't a dial tone."

"Use my phone," I said, grabbing it out and tossing it to him. I wasn't too concerned about my phone because instead of the smartphone that everyone and their brother seemed to have, I had a flip phone. If Tank missed catching it, it would probably just bounce.

Tank dialed and held the phone up to his ear. His eyebrows furrowed together as he looked at it again and punched more buttons. After watching him do it a few times, I realized that we would have to throw in the towel on calling for backup.

"That isn't working either, is it?" I said. Tank shook his head. "The storm must really be wreaking havoc. Knock on wood, but I'm surprised we still have electricity then."

I leaned over and knocked on the wooden table, not wanting to jinx us. Mandy silently stood up and walked out of the door into the entryway. As she pushed back first through the doors, she locked eyes with me, sending me a message that she would get the medicine situation sorted out.

The rest of the room was still quiet. I looked around at everyone else who was still in the dining room. My mother had joined in clearing the table with my father, obviously sticking with decorating the Titanic while it's going down. Linda had made her way around the table and she was clutching Cheryl's hand as they watched. Lyle was hugging Claudia into his chest as she quietly cried. Chelsea was still in her chair, her mouth gaping like a fish. She had her camera sitting on the table, as if she were trying to decide whether to take a picture. But I knew that even Chelsea was not stupid enough to do that.

At this point, I could feel like it was almost too late. I could feel Jake's life slipping through my fingers, almost literally. What a way to start a weekend that was supposed to be about love.

•Chapter Five•

Time seemed to slow down as I sat on the dining room floor with Jake. It felt like no one was doing anything to help. Dawn and I sat holding Jake while everyone else was staring helplessly at us. Thoughts were racing through my head, mainly about where in the world Clark and Anna were with the medicine.

I kept feeling for the pulse on Jake's neck, but it was barely there now. It was shallow and slow and I knew it wouldn't be long before it was completely gone.

"We are losing him," I said, trying to maintain my composure.

"But there wasn't any fish in the dinner," my dad said again as he paused from cleaning the table. He looked befuddled, staring into space as he repeated it again. "There wasn't any fish."

I was getting a bad feeling about this situation. It seemed like a terrible accident, but my dad didn't make mistakes like this, not when it came to the health and safety of B&B guests.

"Can't anyone do anything to help?" I asked.

I was greeted only by silence and quiet sobs as I glanced around the room at everyone's faces. My parents were still clearing the table while Tank and Mandy were trying any phone they could get their hands on. The storm must have knocked out everything.

Linda and Cheryl were still quietly crying together while Joe patted both of their backs. Chelsea was frozen in place, her eyes wide and mouth agape. Lyle and Claudia were walking slowly back and forth between the kitchen door and the door to the rest of the house as if they were trying to find some way to help, but there was nothing for them to do. They almost seemed to be like trapped animals.

Dave was kneeling on the other side of Jake, keeping his fingers on the pulse on Jake's neck. After a few more moments, his heart had slowed down so much it had almost stopped. I locked eyes with Dave and he solemnly nodded before standing up.

"He's gone," Dave said to the room. "Jake is dead."

"What do you mean dead?"

The door to the entryway swung open violently and I turned to see Anna coming back into the room, medicine in hand. She dashed in, shoving Dave aside. Anna ripped the cap off of the needle and jammed it into Jake's outer thigh. Her hair was flowing around her in a wave as she rocked back and forth, counting to ten before she took the medicine pen out of his leg.

"Did that do it?" she asked as she jumped to her feet.

"I'm sorry Anna," I said, feeling no change in his pulse. "I think he is gone."

Anna staggered backward a step and Clark caught her just before she crumpled to the floor. Her long blond hair covered her face as her body started to heave with sobs. Dave rushed to her side and helped Clark carry her out of the dining room.

"Mom, Dad, I think you should see the rest of the guests out to the living room or their rooms, please," I said.

My parents both nodded and set down the dishes they had in their hands. Linda and Cheryl linked arms and scooted out of the dining room with Joe behind them. Lyle and Claudia followed close behind. Chelsea was still standing still and looking puzzled, as if she were sure that Jake was playing some sort of joke.

"Chelsea, leave," I said, a little too gruffly.

"You need to leave now."

She shut her mouth and grabbed her camera, either forgetting to try to take a picture or possibly having some common decency for once. Dawn was still cradling Jake's head. She was stroking his hair tenderly. It was so intimate that I almost felt like I shouldn't be watching.

"Dawn, I think you should go out to the living room also," I said quietly.

Dawn's brown eyes were filled with tears that were about to spill, but she carefully lowered Jake's head to the ground and stood up with the help of one of the dining room chairs. She walked to the door and turned back for one more look before making her way towards the living room.

I stood up and motioned for Mandy and Tank to come closer. I didn't want anyone to overhear me and get the wrong idea and I needed people that I not only could trust, but also were not panicking to help me. I also was glad to have Tank stay here because true to his name, he was built like a tank. No one was going to mess with him even though he was only a teenager still.

"I need the two of you to stay here with Jake's body," I said. "Keep an eye on it and don't let anyone touch that bowl of food."

41

"Do you think someone did this on purpose?" Mandy asked. She always could read me like a book.

"I don't know, but until we are sure we need to make sure to preserve anything that might possibly be a clue," I said. "I'm going into the living room to check on everyone. I will be right back."

The living room was quiet chaos. Clark was sitting with Anna on the couch. She was sobbing and I could hear her muttering into her hands. Dawn was at the other end of the couch, quietly crying and wringing her hands. My father was in the armchair with my mother sitting on the arm. He looked to be in shock over the entire situation.

Linda, Cheryl and their husbands were at the table in the corner, pretending to play a board game. The pieces were out and it appeared they were all taking turns, but the in between was full of whispers and furtive glances.

Lyle, Claudia, and Chelsea were the only ones that appeared to be missing and I assumed they had all gone up to their rooms. I didn't blame them. It had been a weird night and we were still all trapped together with a dead body rapidly cooling in the other room. I decided the first thing I had to do was confirm with my father about the pad thai he had been cooking.

I walked over and settled myself down onto the large, oversize ottoman in front of the armchair. I could hear Anna a little better now and before I started questioning my father, I caught what she was muttering over and over again.

"But I had the medicine," she was telling Clark. "It took a while to find, but I had it. Why didn't it work? I did it exactly the way he showed me."

My heart broke for her. I knew what it was like to lose a spouse unexpectedly and I could feel my own grief for Peter starting to well up but I needed to push it back down, at least for a little bit. I turned my body so that my back was to Anna.

"Dad, I need to ask you a question, but I'd like you to answer quietly, understand?" I said. My dad nodded at me and leaned forward. "Was there anything made with fish in the dinner tonight?"

"No," he answered. It was firm and definitive. "Jake told me both before he got here and when he arrived that he had a severe allergy to fish and that there could be nothing served that contained any sort of fish. I cleared out the kitchen and wiped everything down to make sure that he couldn't react to anything."

"So there is no way that you could have accidentally cross contaminated it?" I asked.

"No, I made sure to use up any and all fish we had late last week so that I could clean the kitchen and disinfect it of any possible allergens before he stayed here," my father said.

His dark eyes were sad and he sat back in the chair with a big sigh as my mother patted his shoulder. I believed him. My father was a bit rough around the edges sometimes, but he would never do anything to endanger someone's life.

I leaned forward and grabbed his hand, giving it a squeeze. He squeezed back once, but let his hand go slack in mine. I could tell he felt guilty and I didn't blame him. He was the cook after all. But now the question was what had happened to Jake's food? I needed to get back to the dining room and figure out what had happened.

•Chapter Six•

Mandy and Tank were both still milling around in the dining room. Jake was still on the dining room floor, although they had grabbed a clean tablecloth out of the kitchen to cover him up. They had also cleared the rest of the table, leaving only the things that had been in Jake's spot.

"My dad says that he knew about Jake's fish allergy and that he went to great lengths to make sure there was no risk of cross-contamination," I said.

"So what happened to make Jake have a reaction like that then?" Tank asked. "Maybe there was something that Dad didn't realize contained fish?"

"Maybe," I said with a shrug. It would make the most sense if this horrible situation was an accident. "Why don't you go in and check everything you can find to see if there is any fish anywhere. Check the fridge, freezer, pantry, everywhere."

Tank nodded and shoved his way through the swinging door. I walked over to Jake's spot at the dinner table and took a look. Nothing looked out of the ordinary and as far as I could remember, it looked exactly like the pad thai I had eaten for dinner. I leaned down and gave his bowl of dinner a good sniff. There was a very faint odor of fish. Was I imagining it? Was all of the talk of fish just making me smell it?

"Mandy, come over here and smell this," I said.

Mandy rolled her eyes at me, but came and inhaled the aroma coming off of the plate of pad thai. She froze for a moment and then took another, deeper inhale. As Mandy straightened back up, her eyes were wide.

"So you smell the fish too?" I asked.

"Yes, but I'm sure that my dinner didn't smell like that," she said. "I definitely would have noticed that smell."

"I'm going to taste it," I said, picking up the fork.

"Are you crazy?" Mandy shrieked, slapping the fork out of my hand. It clattered to the table and Tank stuck his head in the swinging door from the kitchen. We were all a bit jumpy now.

"Everything all right?" he asked, one eyebrow cocked.

"Your crazy sister wants to taste the poisoned pad thai," Mandy said.

"Except it isn't poisoned unless you have

a fish allergy," I said. "Which I don't. At least this time we know where the medicine is just in case I discover I've developed a fish allergy since I ate that tuna melt for lunch yesterday at the Loony Bin."

Mandy rolled her eyes at me and crossed her arms over her chest. I know she was just looking out for me, but gosh it was just like having another annoying sister. I already had two of those, what was one more?

I grabbed the fork off of the table and stabbed a few noodles and vegetables. I smelled them one more time, getting the same aroma of fish that I had before. Gingerly, I brought it to my mouth. I had to admit that Mandy had scared me a little. What if it was poisoned?

Before I could scare myself more, I shoved the entire bite into my mouth and shut my eyes as I chewed. I wanted to focus on the taste, so I chewed slowly.

At first it just tasted like pad thai, but there was something just a bit off about it. The more I chewed, the more it tasted like fish. Jake's reaction to the dinner made more sense as I ate more. The first taste had been normal, but the fishy taste got more and more pronounced as I ate.

"Well, what do you taste?" Mandy asked.

"Fish," I said as I swallowed. "A lot of fish. At first, it tasted fine, but the more I chewed, the more fish I could taste. I'm not sure what is in here, but it is pretty strong."

I used my fork to stir the bowl of food around. As far as I could tell, there weren't any pieces of fish in there. That meant something else had been used to set off Jake's allergic reaction, something a bit more undetectable.

"Come look at this," I said. "I don't actually see any fish in here."

"Let me grab a plate and we can sort through it and look," Mandy said.

She popped into the kitchen for a large plate and another fork and sat down beside me. I tried to forget that there was a dead body behind me on the floor and I made a mental note to try and get through to Officer Max Marcus once the phones were working.

I tried not to smile at the thought of Max as Mandy and I started digging through and sorting the pieces of the pad thai. As we sorted the vegetables from the noodles, I thought about how I had got here. When I moved back to Shady Lake, I had unexpectedly started dating my high school boyfriend again. Max had lost his wife to

cancer just around the same time I had lost
Peter, so it was nice to have someone who
understood the wild roller coaster of grief.

It was also nice to have someone who I
didn't have to get to know. As exciting and
new as everything was with Clark, Max
knew pretty much everything about me. It
was so comfortable to not have to explain
everything to the person I'm dating because
he has already been there for most of it.

Lately, I had been wondering if I'd need
to pick one of them soon. I had told both
Clark and Max that I wasn't looking for a
serious relationship because after Peter, it
was going to take me a while to get back
into wanting something serious. Max was in
the same place as I was, so he understood
and agreed totally.

Clark was a bit of a flirt who enjoyed not
being pinned down. He was the new guy in
town and I often wondered why he chose
me to date. I'm pretty self-critical, so all I
usually see is my lack of proper adult
makeup, inability to dress up, and my
dumpy figure thanks to the self control I do
not have around pizza, donuts, or most
other junk foods. Of course, Clark also
chooses to go out with Chelsea, so he must
not be the best judge of character. Or

Mandy could be right and he could be drawn to my fun personality and pretty face. It pays to have a best friend like Mandy. She may also say that because we are often told that we look like we could be twins.

We finally got to the bottom of the bowl and looked at the plate piled high with food. There was a noodle pile and a vegetable pile, but neither of us found anything that resembled fish.

"I think the only option here is that someone used something like fish sauce to add to this specific bowl of pad thai," Mandy said, sitting back in her chair. "No one else's bowl tasted like fish."

"You're right," I said. "Which means that someone did this on purpose. Now we need to figure out who and why."

I hated to admit that someone had done this to Jake on purpose. He had been a bit of a jerk, but using someone's allergy against them is just plain evil. Food allergies are very serious and should never be used as a weapon.

"Stay here with Jake's body while I check in on Tank," I said.

I pushed through the swinging door to the kitchen and almost ran right into Tank.

He had the door to the pantry cupboard open and was vigilantly turning each item around so that he could read the ingredients label. By the looks of it, he had gotten through about half of the food.

"How is it going in here?" I asked.

"Depending on your view, good or bad," Tank said. "I have found nothing containing fish so far. That's good because it means that Dad didn't do it accidentally. But that's also bad because it means that someone planned to do it and brought something with them."

He was right; it was both good and bad. On one hand, an accidental cross-contamination would have been tragic but it also would have been an accident. On the other hand, having it not be an accident meant that someone had done it on purpose which meant there was a murderer among us.

"Well good, keep looking and let me know if you find anything," I said. "I'm going to try all of the phones again and see if I can get through to Max."

If this really wasn't an accident, I couldn't let anyone in on the fact that I knew. There was something fishy about this entire situation and it wasn't just the pad thai.

•Chapter Seven•

I tried the house phone first, just for good measure. But of course there wasn't even a dial tone when I picked it up. I had a feeling that it was going to take a while to get the landline back in working order since the storm had managed to knock it out right away and the storm wasn't supposed to be done for at least another twenty-four hours.

Next up was my flip phone. I figured if anything could do it, my trusty, dumb phone could. I tapped through and found Max's number and hit the call button. Amazingly, the phone rang a few times before Max's voice came through the other side.

"Hey Sweet Thing," he said, which was a nickname he had called me starting all the way back in high school and could still make me get all ooey gooey inside. "What can I do for you?"

"Are you on duty Max?" I asked, knowing full well that he wasn't. He never would have called me Sweet Thing while he was on duty. Max kept a very strict boundary between his work life and his personal life. "We've had a bit of an incident at the B&B."

"What's wrong," he said. His voice immediately shifted into Officer Marcus mode. "Do you need help Tessa?"

"Well, there's been a, um," I faltered. I had been about to say that we had had an accident, but I wasn't so sure of that. "Let's just say there's been an incident and someone has died."

"What?" Max exclaimed. If it had been possible for him to jump through the phone, I think he would have at that moment. "What do you mean someone has died?"

I tried to briefly describe what had happened, ending with the fact that I didn't think it was actually an accident and that I was trying to figure out what had actually happened.

"I also want to keep it on the down-low because Jake is a celebrity in town," I said. "And I don't want it getting out before we know what actually happened. So don't send any of the town gossips over here, please."

"Okay, here is what I'm going to do," Max said. His voice was starting to cut in and out, just a little. I could tell that I wouldn't be able to keep him on the line forever. "I'm stuck at home, but I will send someone over to you and I will also send an ambulance.

Everyone will be given very firm warnings to zip their lips. But Tessa? It might take a while. This storm is one of the worst I've ever seen and from what I hear, the switchboard is lighting up like a Christmas tree. Obviously it isn't fun to have a dead body there, but that puts you pretty low on the priority list compared to the people stuck in their cars who are trying not to freeze to death."

I sighed because of course he was right. But that was alright because I wanted the time to investigate for myself. The Shady Lake police department did a pretty alright job most of the time but anytime something big happened, they managed to bungle the investigation. They usually would get themselves so set in one line of thinking that they would ignore obvious signs they were wrong, preferring to dig in their heels instead.

"I do think you should move the body," Max said. He was starting to talk faster and faster, trying to make sure he could finish our conversation before the phone dropped our call. "I wouldn't normally say that, but I am for two reasons. First of all, if you can put it somewhere cold it will slow down any decomposition and will maintain any evidence there might be. Second of all, since this is basically a poisoning, there isn't any other physical damage that you may destroy by moving him."

Thank goodness Tank was here because he could help me with that. Hopefully he was old enough to not be scarred for life by moving a dead body with his big sister.

"One last thing," Max said as the phone call started to crackle. We were losing what little connection we had. "You need to keep yourself safe, Tessa."

"I will, you know that."

"I just don't want to lose you," Max said. He knew full well that I managed to get myself into trouble more frequently than any normal adult does. "I love..."

And with that, the phone call died. Just my luck. The first time we were going to tell each other that we loved each other since we got back together and we were thwarted. I stared at the phone in my hand, wondering if that was some sort of omen from the universe.

"I love you too," I whispered.

"What?" Mandy asked from her perch next to Jake's dead body. "Never mind, just tell me the game plan."

I ran her through what needed to be done

and we moved on to the first course of action, which was to help Tank finish looking through the food so that we could check that off of our list. As we cleared out the fridge and pantry, I told Tank the plan also.

As the oldest of five kids, I'm used to being the biggest and the one in charge. I also am used to each of my siblings being stuck at a certain age in my mind. In my mind, Tank is perpetually four years old. Obviously he is well over six feet tall and weighs about three times as much as me, but I still always think of him as being so young.

But after I told him the plan, there was a moment where it dawned on me that he was seventeen and practically an adult. His eyes were serious as he looked at me, ready to be a partner in my crazy investigative plan and not just some little brother who follows me around.

"So I'm assuming I'm the one who has to carry the corpse?" he said. "Where do you want him?"

"Well I can help you," I said, knowing full well that having Tank do it by himself would be much easier than having me pretend to help him. The height difference alone meant Tank would have to practically crawl on his knees for me to be of any help. "But I was thinking we could put him on a tarp out on the back porch."

"You and Mandy get the tarp and some blankets and I will get the body," he said.

Tank knelt down and gently put his arms underneath Jake's rapidly cooling body. He stood up slowly, being careful to give the dead body the respect it deserved. I walked to the door to the entryway hall and peeked out. The last thing we needed was someone to see us moving the body and go to pieces. It was empty and I could still hear voices up in the living room.

"Mandy, go stand in the doorway to the living room and make sure no one comes out while we are moving him," I said.

Mandy casually walked up the hallway and leaned against the door frame, careful not to make it look like she was guarding them even though she definitely was. Seeing her calm demeanor made me wish she would help me with these investigations more often. Not that I necessarily loved getting roped into these situations all the time, but I did enjoy true crime podcasts and books so it was kind of exciting to put my skills to good use every once in a while.

Mandy, on the other hand, got too freaked out by true crime stuff. I had recommended her my favorite podcast once but the first time they mentioned something that wasn't even that gory, she deleted it off of her phone and swore never to listen again. So her usefulness was extremely limited. In fact, the only reason she was being this helpful now was surely because she was stuck here for an undetermined amount of time.

I nodded my head back to Tank and held the door open. He slowly lumbered up to the door, turning to make extra sure that he wouldn't slam Jake's head into the door frame. After he passed me, I quietly pushed the door shut so that no one would hear and get suspicious.

Tank's large frame walked slowly and steadily down the hallway with Jake's head and feet the only things visible, dangling over his arms on either side. I already knew there would be a tarp on the back porch, so I wasn't worried about running ahead to find one.

"What are you doing?"

A voice from the staircase startled me and I turned to see Lyle coming down from his room. His eyes were wide and he was grasping the handrail of the staircase so hard that I could see his knuckles turning white.

Tank turned and looked at me. His face that had been so serious and sure had now softened to look more like the childlike face I was used to. He was worried and looking to me for some help. I waved my hand, shooing him towards the back porch as I bounded up the stairs just in time to grab Lyle's arm as he sat down hard on one of the stairs.

"It's okay Mr. Roberts," I said. "We were told by the emergency dispatchers to put Jake's body somewhere cold to help slow any decomposition. We are moving him to the back porch until someone can get through the storm to help us with him."

I cringed at the words I had picked, but I plowed on with my polite, but somewhat stern, customer service voice. From his perch on the stairs, Lyle's face crumpled. This must be the first time he had been so close to a dead body and it seemed to really be throwing him for a loop.

"Maybe you could go wait in the living room with the others, Mr. Roberts?"

I made it more of a command than a

suggestion, and as he showed signs of starting to stand up, I grabbed his arm and helped him to his feet. Tank was almost to the porch door; I needed to help him.

"Mr. Roberts, I'll be in to talk to everyone in a moment," I said. "Please make your way to the front room."

I walked backwards, making sure that he was on his way. As soon as he rounded the corner into the living room, I grabbed the door knob to the porch and pushed it open.

The porch was freezing cold and the wind was still whipping snow everywhere outside. The porch was a three season porch, so it had no insulation from the winter temperatures. I shivered as I grabbed a tarp off of a ramshackle shelf that stood on one side of the door. It held all sorts of random outdoor things and I was glad that the tarp I assumed would be there was still there.

It was so cold that I started to shiver uncontrollably as I spread the tarp on the wooden floor of the porch. Once it was down, Tank knelt down and together we spread Jake out on the tarp. The porch was pretty weather tight, but I didn't want to take any chances.

"Tank, go grab a blanket to cover him

with," I said.

Tank ducked out the door and for a moment, I was alone with the body. I took Jake's cold hand in mine and gave it a squeeze. His face was still a bit swollen and red. It was odd to be with someone who had just died because he looked like he could wake up at any moment and be upset that he was on the cold back porch.

"I promise that I will find who did this to you," I whispered.

There had been a few times now that I had found a dead body and felt compelled to investigate, but this was the first time that I had seen someone actually die. That fact was weighing heavy on my mind and I was not going to take that for granted. I was going to solve this and figure out who would do this to Jake Crawford.

•Chapter Eight•

After Tank and I covered Jake with a blanket, we joined Mandy in the doorway to the living room. Everyone looked just like I had left them, except Lyle had come down to the living room. We were only missing two people now and I wanted everyone together so I could get them up to speed on what was happening.

"Mandy, can you run upstairs and get Chelsea and Claudia down here?" I asked.

With a nod, Mandy dashed up the stairs and I could hear her knocking on the door one of the doors at the top of the stairs. I glanced around the living room, wondering who had been the one to poison Lyle. It was eerie to know that someone here was a killer. Someone had taken advantage of Jake's allergy and used it against him.

I felt someone grab my elbow and turned to see Mandy was back with Chelsea and Claudia following close behind. I moved aside and let them into the living room. No one was paying much attention to us or the people we had just brought down.

"Mandy, Tank, I need you to do something important," I whispered. "When I tell them that Jake's death was not an accident, I need you to help me see how everyone reacts. That will be a major clue for us. Mandy, you watch the table where they are playing a game and Tank, you watch Lyle and Claudia."

They both nodded at me, ready to help the investigation. Tank cleared his throat loudly and everyone looked towards us. There was a startled look that seemed to be shared by almost everyone here. I don't think anyone was suspecting that Jake's allergy attack was anything but an accident. I felt bad that I was about to rip their feeling of peace away from them.

"If I could please have everyone's attention, I have a few things to say," I said.

The wind was howling outside, blowing so much snow past the window that we could hardly see the bird feeders that were placed in the yard just a few feet away. It was going to take a while for any help to be here, so I needed to make sure not to scare anyone or freak out whoever did this to Jake.

"First of all, everyone should know that I have been in contact with the police," I said. "They are sending an ambulance and police officer, but we should be prepared to not see them for a while. Obviously this storm is extremely bad and we are low on the priority list."

"A dead body is low on the priority list?" Lyle yelled. "That is incredibly rude and demeaning to the memory of Jake."

A sob erupted from Anna, who until then had been quietly crying. Dawn scooted down the couch to put her arm tentatively around Anna's shoulders.

"What they mean is that there are people stuck in their cars literally freezing to death," I said, glaring at Lyle. "Rescuing them is higher on the priority list than taking care of someone who is already dead and cannot come back to life."

Lyle shrank back towards the wall, sheepishly pretending like he was looking through the books on the bookshelf. His wife, Claudia, was giving him a look, obviously confused about his outburst.

"Either way, we were advised to move Jake's body to somewhere cold to slow down any decomposition," I said, looking anywhere but at Anna as she let out another sob. I understood, I really did. But I had to relay the news. "We have moved his body to the back porch and we ask that no one bother the body until the ambulance arrives to take him away."

This was met with nods and some murmurs of agreement. I don't think anyone would bother Jake's body. He was dead and he hadn't died in some sort of way that left evidence, so I wouldn't have to worry about the killer disturbing the body. At least, I don't think I would have to worry about it.

"I have one other important thing to say," I said. "Jake obviously died because of an allergic reaction to fish, but I'm going to go ahead and tell you that it was not an accident."

The small amount of noise in the room dropped off immediately and everyone's eyes were on me. Dawn still had her arm around Anna and they both had tears in their eyes, but they both were staring at me with their mouths open and their eyes wide. My parents were both turned around in the chair and I could see exactly what they were doing. They were searching my face, trying to see if I was lying or playing some sort of sick joke.

Annoyingly, Chelsea was standing next to Clark and when I revealed that this incident was not an accident, she clutched onto him like she was about to fall over. I tried not to scowl as I looked away. Chelsea hated that Clark and I went out because she wanted him all to herself.

"One person here decided to put fish in Jake's dinner, knowing full well that he was allergic," I said. "I don't know why, but I do know that it was not an accident."

I paused, trying to decide what to say next. Whoever killed Jake did so for some totally unknown reason. If I knew the reason, I would know how to address the situation. But I didn't want to anger whoever did it. We were all stuck here during this winter storm for an undetermined amount of time and I didn't need to anger someone who had already killed one person.

After one more glance around the room, I decided that I needed to take the lead. If no one took the lead, chaos may break out. So I made the split-second decision to step up.

"I want to assure you all, especially whoever did this to Jake, that I will find out who did this," I said. "I will figure it out and I will make sure you are turned over to the police. Mandy and Tank will be assisting me and we will be questioning everyone to see if anyone noticed anything. All we ask is for your cooperation. Thank you."

I walked out into the hallway and as soon as I was out of view of the living room, I took a deep breath and bent down, putting my hands on my knees. At the ripe old age of thirty I felt both like I was technically an adult, but also that I was play-acting as an adult. It didn't help that I was living with my parents.

A hand pressed lightly on my back and I turned to see Mandy standing beside me. She didn't have to say anything. I could see through her expression that she was cheering me on and telling me that she believed in me. She had always been my biggest cheerleader and even though she was chomping on a piece of gum as she did it, I appreciated the gesture.

I thought a cup of coffee was in order. Of course at this point in the evening, I'd have to make decaf. But I just couldn't kick my coffee habit and a decaf cup was better than caffeinated.

"Mandy, will you go into the living room and see if anyone would like a cup of decaf coffee or a cup of tea?" I asked. "I'm going to head to the kitchen and put a pot on."

"Yes, I can do that," she said, giving me a small scowl.

I seemingly lacked that little angel on my

shoulder that talks me out of doing things I shouldn't, like eating three donuts in a day or drinking coffee at night. Mandy takes the place of that angel. She doesn't judge but does discourage. And honestly, I like that and I need that.

I headed through the dining room, trying not to think about the fact that someone had died there just over an hour ago, and walked through the swinging door to the kitchen. Unfortunately, I walked right into my worst nightmare.

As the door pushed open, I could see Clark and Chelsea locked in a passionate embrace. They were holding each other so tightly that they were almost melding into one person. As soon as they realized that they weren't alone anymore, they jumped apart, trying to pretend like they hadn't just been making out in the kitchen of a bed and breakfast.

At first, they didn't realize who had walked in on them, but as soon as they saw it was me, each of their faces flipped immediately to a different emotion. Clark's face automatically blushed itself into a look of shame while Chelsea's face twisted itself up into an evil sneer.

"Really?" I said, trying not to get too loud.

Just what I didn't need was to have everyone think that someone else had died. "In my own house?"

Chelsea started to giggle and I couldn't tell if it was a giggle of embarrassment or glee, but I had a feeling that it was a bit of both.

"Oops," she said with a smile. Chelsea briefly put her hand on Clark's arm and when he shrugged it off, she slipped back through the door to the living room.

Clark and I were left staring at each other. I didn't have to tell him how I felt because I could feel that it was written across my face. Judging by his expression, he was feeling really bad about it. But it was a little too late for that. He should have thought about it before he started kissing another girl in my house.

"Please leave the kitchen," I said as flatly as I could manage. "I'm making coffee and I don't want to talk to you right now."

Clark ran his hand through his hair, looking too darn handsome and for a moment making me wonder if I should just forget about what I had just walked in on. But after a beat, I realized that I was not the kind of woman to just sit back and let a man disrespect me. Absolutely not. Clark would not be getting off that easy.

Once he realized that I was serious and not going to just laugh it off, he sheepishly walked by me, avoiding my gaze. Clark was a flirt for sure and I was okay with him going out with Chelsea and other women, just not in my house.

I turned my attention back to the coffeepot, throwing together a pot of decaf before I grabbed a cookie to eat while I watched the coffee brew.

Recently, I had been wondering about my true thoughts about being with Clark. It was fun and exciting, but when I compared him to Max, Clark lost pretty much every time. Maybe I need to think about ending this whole "dating for fun" time of my life and move back into a "dating seriously" time. The only thing that scared me is what would happen if Max wasn't ready to date seriously.

•Chapter Nine•

Mandy came back in shortly with a list of coffee and tea orders from the living room. Hopefully it isn't weird to call your totally an adult best friend/almost sister cute because Mandy totally was. She came bustling back in with a little pad of paper and a pencil up above her ear like she was playing waitress. It was funny though because everyone said Mandy and I looked a lot a like but while I could agree that Mandy was cute, I would not say the same about myself.

"Okay, what's wrong?" she asked as soon as she saw my face, which I was stuffing with cookie.

I explained what I had walked into and she gave a sympathetic look. Mandy had been sort of living vicariously through me because she has been with her boyfriend for over ten years now. Shortly after I left for college, she started dating Trevor and they had been together ever since. I used to think he was a good for nothing, but he had bucked up and shown he wasn't the same skater boy he had been in high school. He was back in school now besides working his full-time job as an emergency dispatcher.

I waved off the sympathy after a moment and stuck out my hand for the list of drink orders. Together, Mandy and I poured everyone's drinks and arranged a plate of cookies on a tray. Before we brought the refreshments into the living room, I told her I thought we should make a plan.

"The first two people we need to talk to are Anna and Dawn," I said. "Obviously Anna because she couldn't find the medicine and Dawn had a very intense reaction to Jake's death. Plus, both of them were helping to serve dinner."

"Okay," Mandy said. "Whatever you say, boss."

We each grabbed a tray and brought it out to the living room. Everyone still seemed to be sitting exactly where I had left them a while ago. Mandy and I wound our way around the room, giving everyone the drinks they ordered and offering cookies.

I ended my trip around the living room by sitting down next to Anna. Her eyes were ringed with red and her long blond hair was covering her like a security blanket. She didn't look at me right away; she was staring off into space and I couldn't really blame her. She had just lost her husband.

"Anna, I'd like you to come with me," I said quietly. "I'll bring your tea to the kitchen if you'll just follow, please."

She stared up through the curtain of hair and gave me such a blank look that I wasn't sure she had actually heard me. But as I stood up, she did too and together we walked to the kitchen with Mandy following behind. As I held the door for them, I glanced at Tank. He was stationed in the doorway and he gave me a nod. He was keeping an eye out here in the living room.

In the kitchen, I pulled a chair out at the table and motioned Anna to sit down. As she sat down, she took her smartphone out of her pocket and put it next to her on the table. She seemed a bit obsessed with it, which just made me glad once again to have traded mine in. Mandy and I took a seat across from her. She looked like she wanted to keep crying, but she had run out of tears at the moment.

"Anna, I know this is a really hard time and you just lost Jake, but I need to ask you just a few questions," I said. "I'll keep it brief, but I want you to tell me anything you know."

Anna looked a bit surprised but nodded her head slightly, making her hair shimmer like a wave.

"First of all, do you have any idea who would want to do this to Jake?" I asked. From the true crime stuff I have watched, it is best to start with something pretty general and work towards the specific. If I was lucky, maybe it would make less work for me.

"No, I mean, not anyone specifically," Anna said. She took a small sip from her tea cup. "Jake was not the nicest, even to me. But I can't think of anyone who would actually want to kill him. Besides, he kept his fish allergy mostly a secret. I think deep down, he always worried something like this would happen."

Anna's voice cracked just a little and Mandy hurried over to the counter to grab her a tissue. Anna took it gratefully and wiped her face before sipping a little bit more of her tea.

"So what you are saying is that not just anyone would know about this allergy, so it would have to be someone close to him," I said. "Like his wife? You haven't been married long, but how is your marriage going so far?"

"Tessa," Mandy hissed as a few tears and a sob escaped from Anna. I glanced her way, but if Mandy didn't understand the whole "good cop, bad cop" routine, she was about to learn.

"Our marriage was going as well as I thought it would," Anna said. She seemed to be picking her words carefully. "Like I said, Jake was not always nice and honestly I think I could have found someone nicer. But what Jake did was allow me to follow my dreams. He knew I wanted to pursue a career as a dancer and he let me. When you start out, it isn't all sunshine and daisies. A lot of times, I would go weeks between paying gigs and would have to spend money in the meantime on dance classes, new outfits for auditions, a personal trainer, that sort of thing. He didn't mind that I didn't have a steady job because he made enough money for both of us. Plus, I was pretty and willing to put up with his more childish tantrums. It may not have been the best sort of relationship, but it was working for us."

Well I couldn't argue with her on that front. The older I got, the more I was realizing that a relationship didn't have to make any sense as long as the people in it were happy. I took a sip of coffee and grabbed a cookie off of the plate in the middle of the table, pushing it towards Anna who politely refused.

"But you were clearly unhappy to be here in Shady Lake," I said, remembering all of the time she had been spending on her phone and computer.

Anna gave a sigh and grudgingly took a cookie. She took a bite and stared out the window at the ever-blowing snow while she chewed. Looking out at the blizzard, I could understand how this trip to the frozen tundra would not be exactly what this California girl would be looking forward to.

"Shady Lake is a cute little town," Anna said. "And I was happy to meet Jake's grandparents and spend time with his parents. But it is hard to leave California, especially during Valentine's Day. I had been hoping to have a very romantic evening."

Anna glanced around nervously and poked the button on her phone, lighting the screen up so she could check for notifications. When there was nothing new there, she pushed it away from her a bit and sighed.

"There is another reason too, isn't there?" I asked. "Another reason why you didn't want to come so far away from California? What is it you are always doing on your phone?"

Mandy gave me a little shove and when I glanced at her, she bulged her eyes at me. She wanted me to stop pushing Anna so far, but I really didn't think I had done too much. I was just trying to get as much information as I could.

"Yes, there was another reason," Anna said. She paused and took another sip of tea. I could tell she was thinking about what exactly she should tell us. She must have decided we were trustworthy. "And before I tell you, let me just say that Jake knew and he didn't mind as long as I was discrete."

Mandy let out a little yelp and it was my turn to shove her a little bit. Hopefully Anna wouldn't think Mandy was being judgmental because whatever it was she needed to be discrete about, I needed to know about it.

"I may as well tell you because I want to make sure you know everything," Anna said. "I have a boyfriend back home in California. His name is Lark. Jake knew about our relationship and was okay with it. In fact we had discussed him having a girlfriend also, if he found the right girl."

Anna looked in my eyes and I could tell that she wasn't lying. I appreciated her honesty, but there was no way for me to check if Jake knew about Lark and what he thought of the entire situation.

"I have one more question," I said. "When you went to find Jake's medicine, it took a very long time. What happened?"

While some of my questioning had taken her away from the what had happened, this plopped her right back in the life-altering mess that had happened earlier in the evening. She teared up again as she described what happened.

"I told Jake he should always carry the epinephrine if he was going to eat," Anna said. "But he kind of just laughed me off as being too worried and said that it was always near enough. He keeps it in a little carrying pouch that he can bring with in a briefcase or backpack. But when I went upstairs, it was like the pouch had been moved. I finally found it in the top drawer of the nightstand."

"And that was odd?" I asked.

"Definitely," Anna said. "He never would have put it somewhere like the nightstand where it could have been forgotten. He always left it in one of his bags. It was like someone had moved it, but I don't think anyone else knew about it."

With that, she collapsed back into sobs, the tears flowing again. I reached over the table and grabbed her hand. I knew what she was going through and the pain of losing Peter felt like a fresh wound. But I took a deep breath and tried to put a bandage on it because I just couldn't deal with it and a murder investigation right now.

"I'm sorry for what happened, Anna," I said. "But I promise that we will figure out what happened to Jake."

She looked in my eyes and nodded. Mandy stood up and helped Anna through the kitchen and up to her room. We both figured she had been through enough tonight and should be able to get some rest if she needed to.

As I waited for Mandy to come back, I thought through what Anna had said. Someone had moved the epinephrine. Had it been the same person who had put the fish in Jake's bowl? It had to be someone close to Jake who knew about not only the allergy, but also the pouch where he kept his medicine. But who was as close to him as his wife? Had Anna been the one to do it? If so, maybe she should go into acting instead of dancing.

•Chapter Ten•

When Mandy came back into the kitchen,
I could tell by her face that she was already
a little overwhelmed. While she had helped
me figure things out when I investigated
mysteries previously, usually she just
provided more of a listening ear and some
moral support. This time she was totally in
the investigation and she was already
feeling the enormity of it.

She sat back down and took a cookie,
which was definitely another sign that
something was different. For someone that
works in a donut shop, Mandy has
extraordinary willpower when it comes to
sweets.

"So, do you think Anna was telling the
truth?" Mandy asked as she nibbled on the
cookie.

"Yes, I do," I said. "Which is a bit
confusing because she is the one who makes
the most sense to be the killer. But I could
tell that she was being sincere. She even told
us about her boyfriend, which she didn't
have to do. She seemed genuinely upset
about losing Jake."

"But couldn't her boyfriend also be her

motive to kill Jake?" Mandy asked. "Maybe marriage was not what she thought it would be and she just wants to be with her boyfriend."

"Sure, it could be," I said with a shrug. "And it would make sense because from what Anna said, whoever did this to Jake must have been intimately close to him. He hid his allergy and whoever did this must have hidden his medicine so that he wouldn't get it in time."

We quietly drank our coffee and tea and munched on our cookies while the wind blew by the window outside. I couldn't believe how bad this storm was. I couldn't even see the trees that were just out the window. Max had said this was the worst storm he had ever seen and I had to agree with him. Thinking of Max, I hoped he was getting someone out here soon.

"So if we can't add people to the list of suspects, are there people we can take off of the suspect list?" Mandy asked.

"Yes, I actually think we can take Linda, Dave, Cheryl, and Joe off of the suspect list because they don't seem to know Jake besides the fact that he is from Shady Lake," I said. "They also didn't have anything to do with the dinner. Same with my mother."

"On that note, we can take Clark and Chelsea off of the suspect list too," Mandy said. I had to agree, as much as I was feeling like pinning it all on them would be great retribution at the moment.

"I think we can take Claudia off of the list, but Lyle needs to stay on because he helped bring the dinner plates out," I said. "Same with Dawn and my father. They all were in contact with dinner."

"Didn't Anna bring dinner plates out also?" Mandy asked.

"Yes," I said with a sigh. "I suppose we should leave her on the list, although towards the bottom because I really have a gut feeling that she did not do it."

So there was our suspect list: my father, Anna, Lyle, and Dawn. The only one who we knew had a connection and could have done it was Anna and if there was anything I'd learned from doing a little amateur investigation was that going with your gut was almost always the right thing to do. And my gut was saying that she had not done it.

I was about to speak up in Anna's defense again when suddenly all of the lights went out and Mandy and I were plunged into darkness. I was immediately enveloped in crippling anxiety. My breathing was shallow and I tried to take deep breaths, but it wasn't working. My stomach felt like it was eating itself and I was starting to shiver.

A hand suddenly landed on my arm and I jumped before I turned and saw Mandy kneeling next to me. She had turned on the little flashlight on her smartphone and it was lighting up a little area of the linoleum tile on the kitchen floor. I stared at the spot that was lit up, trying to focus my attention on it and push back the fear of the dark.

"Tell me where the nearest flashlight is, Tessa," Mandy said, her voice flat and calm.

"Basement stairs," I managed to say.

Mandy squeezed my shoulder before she stood up and dashed towards the door to the basement. I closed my eyes and tried to focus on the facts of the case while I waited for Mandy. Through my eyelids, I could see a light approaching and when I opened my eyes, Mandy was holding the butt of the flashlight towards me.

As soon as the cold, metal flashlight was in my hand, my anxiety immediately dropped back down to a manageable level. I took a moment and did some deep breathing while I shone the flashlight slowly into each corner of the kitchen.

"Let's go to the living room," Mandy said.

She grabbed my arm and looped hers through it before helping to lead me into the living room. Thankfully, the fireplace already had a roaring fire which was lighting up most of the room. Everyone was still in the room except for my parents, who I assumed were doing damage control by checking the electric panel and gathering candles and flashlights.

I saw that Chelsea and Clark appeared to be cuddling on the sofa and as I came in, Clark sheepishly tried to push Chelsea away as Chelsea tried to pull Clark closer. They ended up in a sort of odd, wrestling match that I turned away from so that I didn't have to watch it. Instead, I walked over to where Tank was still stationed in the doorway.

"Are you okay?" he asked before I could even open my mouth. He knew about my fear of the dark after one night when I woke up in a panic and found that my bedside flashlight wasn't working anymore. In my panic, I had started to yell and Tank had come to my rescue.

"I'm fine," I said. "Mandy helped me get my flashlight. How are things going in here?"

"Well, the lights going out was certainly something, although I can't say it was a surprise to me," Tank said.

We had grown up in this old house and we were used to the power going out frequently. Any time there was supposed to be a winter storm, we bought up an entire supply of candles and batteries for flashlights. In the summer, we kept a tote of candles and batteries in the basement for severe storms and tornado warnings. Sometimes the power would just go out for no reason, so it was all old hat to us.

I peeked around Tank's hulking figure and saw my parents in the entryway. I squeezed my way past him and walked over to where my parents were setting up and lighting candles. When we had been little and the power had gone out, we were each given a flashlight and my mother would carry around a camping lantern.

But now that we had a bed and breakfast, my parents had gone all out. Every surface in the entryway and hallway had lit candles on top of it. The entire area glowed with candlelight. It looked like we had planned this romantic atmosphere for Valentine's Day weekend.

"Tessa, are you okay?" my father asked, looking concerned when he noticed me. "We knew you were with Mandy and that she would take care of you, otherwise we would have come in immediately."

I smiled, knowing that was true. My father frequently supported my flashlight habit by buying large amounts of batteries for me. He had always been kind of a sucker for his firstborn daughter. But then, he was kind of a sucker for all of his children. My father may act big and tough sometimes, but he has a soft heart inside.

"I'm fine Dad," I said, grabbing a few candles and finding more spaces to put them as my father followed me to light them. "You're right. Mandy took care of me."

"If you two are alright, I'm going back in the living room," my mother said.

We waved her off as we continued lighting candles. I suddenly had an idea and ran over to the stairs, setting a candle on the very edge of the staircase on every other step. My father stood looking for a moment before starting to light them for me.

"Dad, I had a question for you," I said. I knew this would be a perfect time to ask him about Jake's allergic reaction because my mother wasn't around. She never approved of me investigating anything and I'm sure she thought I should butt out this time also, even though someone had to investigate and obviously the police couldn't get here yet. I've always heard that the first few hours are the most important when investigating a crime and I wasn't going to waste them.

"So like I said before, Mandy and I are pretty sure this was not an accident," I said. "So you don't have to worry because we didn't find anything with fish in it in the kitchen."

My dad let out a sigh of relief, even though he still looked worried. I didn't blame him. Even though he hadn't accidentally killed Jake, someone had still died in the bed and breakfast.

"But I wanted to ask if you saw anyone acting suspiciously or anyone who came in the kitchen and was curious about what you were cooking?" I asked, placing the last few candles on the top stairs.

My dad finished lighting the candles and motioned me to follow him. When we got back to the main floor, my dad sat down behind the welcome desk and I stood next to him.

"Honestly Tessa, most of the guests were acting suspiciously," he said. "I know it is pretty special that Jake is in town and chose to stay here, but it is like everyone went a little nuts. I have overheard more whispered arguments in the past two days than I have in the past month."

"Who was arguing?" I asked.

"Everyone," my dad said. "Jake and his wife. Jake and Dawn. Jake and Lyle. Lyle and Claudia. Lyle and Dawn. Jake and Chelsea. Anna and Chelsea. Honestly, it is like some sort of very quiet, very secretive soap opera over here. I just thought Jake was pretty high-maintenance. And he was, but obviously there must have been something else going on too."

He was definitely right about that. But what was going on? The only thing I knew so far was that Anna had a boyfriend back in California, but was that what she and Jake had been arguing about? I would have to ask her.

"Tessa?" my dad said, snapping me out of my thoughts. "Are you going to be alright tonight? Do you have enough batteries and flashlights?"

"I think so," I said. "Plus Mandy will be

sleeping in my room, so I will have all of my bases covered."

My dad's shoulders relaxed down as he let out a big exhale. Even though I was firmly in my adult years, he would never stop worrying about me.

"One more thing," my dad said. "You asked about who was in the kitchen while I was cooking dinner. Everyone was. That was another strange thing about these last few days. The same people that have been doing all of the arguing have been so overly curious and concerned about what I was cooking that I can't keep them out of the kitchen. Every time I turn around in there, someone else is looking over my shoulder."

Oh boy, well that doesn't really help. I thought maybe my dad would have noticed one person who really stuck out for being oddly involved in the kitchen, but of course that would be much too easy. So for now, we are stuck in a blizzard in the bed and breakfast with multiple people who could be the killer. I just hope we can get a little help from the police soon.

•Chapter Eleven•

The living room was quietly bustling. The fire in the fireplace was crackling and the two couples at the table in the corner were actually playing the board game now instead of just pretending. Quiet conversations floated around along with the sound of book pages turning and game pieces moving, everything set against the background noise of screeching wind from outside the windows.

With the exception of Anna, who I assumed had gone to bed after we had talked to her, everyone was still there. I wondered if they were wanting to go to their rooms to get away from whoever was the killer, scared that they may be next. Of course that meant that unless the killer was Anna, they were probably sitting in the same room as the killer. But it provided a false sense of security to have everyone around and I can't say I blame them.

Mandy was now sitting on the sofa with Clark and Chelsea, who were both looking incredibly uncomfortable. Good, they shouldn't be able to get comfortable. I tried not to laugh as Mandy winked at me, knowing full well what she was doing.

I had one more person that I needed to talk to tonight and that was Dawn. She was sitting in the corner of the living room in an armchair, paging through one of the books from the bookshelf. I walked over and knelt down next to her.

"Dawn, I'd like you to come with me into the kitchen please," I said.

At first, I thought she may be ignoring me, but after a moment, she shut her book and nodded at me. We both stood up and went through the door to the kitchen with Mandy following close behind. We settled ourselves at the table and Mandy brought over a plate of cookies.

"Would either of you like anything to drink?" Mandy asked, ever the perfect hostess despite the fact that we were actually in my house and I had totally neglected to ask. Both of us shook our heads.

"Dawn, I had a few questions I wanted to ask you about Jake," I said. I thought back to how she held him as he died. It had been so intimate and comfortable that they couldn't have just been strangers.

"Jake and I used to be married," Dawn said flatly.

Mandy and I both turned and looked at each other wide-eyed. For a moment, I wondered if I hadn't heard her properly. Honestly, I figured that she was going to reveal that she was obsessed with him or that she was his agent or something. The fact that they had been married was something I had not seen coming.

"Umm, okay," I said, taking a bite of cookie so I could think about where to go from there. By the time I finished chewing, I had thought of another question. "So why were you here?"

"Honestly, I came because I wanted to talk to him about our divorce settlement," Dawn said. "I didn't like the terms and I think I deserved a little bit more. See, I've gotten myself into just a little bit of credit card debt because I was accustomed to a much better lifestyle than I can afford now. So I came to ask him for more."

"So you crashed part of his honeymoon on Valentine's Day weekend to ask for more money?" Mandy asked. When she put it like that, it was pretty terrible.

Dawn was scrunching her mouth around like there was something gross in there that she was trying to chew up. I had a feeling that she had gotten herself into one of those situations that sounds like a great plan, but turns out that it is awful. Like the time I tried one of those trendy pixie haircuts in my early twenties, somehow forgetting that my hair takes forever to grow out. Although my mistake was just my awkward hair and didn't have anything to do with someone dying.

"I guess you could say that," Dawn said. "But I didn't bother Anna. In fact, Anna doesn't even know Jake and I had been married to each other. I didn't want to bother her, so I've been steering clear of her. But yesterday she was busy on her computer in the living room and I was able to talk to Jake a little bit."

"And how did that go?" Mandy demanded. I tried not to look surprised, but I got the feeling that Mandy's disapproval of Dawn's plan meant that she wasn't going to play the good cop role.

Dawn squirmed in her chair as I took another bite of cookie. I was trying not to munch on it, but it was hard not to while watching this scene play out.

"It didn't go well," Dawn said. "He was upset that I was here and demanded I leave right away. I told him that I would try not to bother him, but that I had a room booked all weekend and I hoped we could talk it out like adults."

"This is a tough question, but why did you and Jake get divorced?" Mandy asked. Her face had softened into the one that usually got people to spill their guts. She had one of those faces that people just want to talk to.

"Jake's star was rising fast and he thought I was dragging it down," Dawn said. "I wasn't willing to change who I was to be what he thought I should be."

I searched her face for any sign that she was upset about her divorce, but there was no sadness there. I can't say I blame her for potentially being happy to be rid of the jerk. Immediately, I felt a little guilty about thinking ill of the dead.

"I have one more question for you," I said, pushing on. "I'm going to assume that you knew about Jake's allergy and the medicine he carried for it?"

"Of course I did," Dawn said. "He walked me through what to do if he ever had an allergic reaction, but apparently he forgot to do that for his ditzy new wife."

Mandy opened her mouth and I quickly nudged her arm. It appeared more likely that Anna knew what to do, but hadn't been able to do that. But until we knew for sure, I didn't want Mandy to drop any valuable information on a suspect.

"Thanks Dawn," I said. "If you can think of anything else that has to do with Jake or his death, please let us know."

Dawn nodded and quickly stood up, her chair sliding across the linoleum with a squeal. She marched her way back into the living room, leaving Mandy and I at the kitchen table. I put my hand out to grab another cookie, but paused mid-way, trying to remember how many I had eaten so far tonight. Mandy took that opportunity to grab the plate and move it over to the counter. It's great to have a best friend that will also function as your willpower.

"Well, what did you think about all of that?" I asked Mandy. I might be good at finding clues, but Mandy was good at reading people and I needed to rely on her skills if this web of relationships got any more tangled.

"I have to say that I did not think she would tell us she had been married to Jake," Mandy said. "She is pretty good at playing her feelings close to the vest. I do think it is obvious that she doesn't like Anna."

"Well, I get the feeling that Anna is

everything Dawn wasn't," I said. "Jake seemed pretty into playing the role of Hollywood star and Anna certainly has the looks and personality that he needed for the wife of a celebrity."

Just another reason to dislike Jake. He was obviously a full-of-himself jerk, but if he really did throw away his marriage to Dawn just to marry someone more "Hollywood," that's pretty low.

A glance at the battery powered clock on the wall told me that it was getting late. Mandy and I walked into the living room and once again, everyone seemed to be frozen in time where we had left them before. I decided to take charge.

"Excuse me, could I get everyone's attention?" I asked. Slowly, everyone's eyes turned towards me as if they had all been in a daze.

"It is getting late and I would like everyone to retire to their rooms," I said. "I will contact the police again and see if we have an estimate on what time they will be able to come, but until morning I'd like everyone to stay in their rooms."

"We aren't prisoners," Lyle said. His face was turning pink and he started to splutter as he talked. "What gives you the right to lock us in our rooms?"

"No one is locking you in your room except you," my father said, standing up from his armchair. He wasn't a big man, but his steady confidence was a force of nature. "We are simply asking everyone to stay in their rooms for their own safety. When the police get here, we will let everyone know and anyone who is still awake will be allowed to come back out. But until we figure out who did this, it would be best for everyone to stay in their room."

Lyle's face was slowly darkening from pink to red, but Claudia put her hand on his arm and after a glance at her disapproving face, he kept his mouth shut.

"We have a flashlight for each of you," my father continued on. "And we have lit the entryway and stairway. As soon as all of you guests are in your rooms, we will blow out the candles down here until morning when hopefully the storm will be winding down and the power will be back."

"Thank you for working with us," my mother said. "Obviously we can't control the weather or the fact that the power is out, but we are trying our best to get through it."

Slowly, the guests started to get up and head to their rooms. Dave and Joe collected their flashlights while their wives put the board game they had been playing away. Claudia and Dawn put their books back on the book shelf. Chelsea was in a whispered discussion with Clark and from what I could hear, he was staunchly refusing to sleep in her room, no matter how scared she was.

"I just don't think it is right for me to stay there even if I am sleeping on the sofa," Clark whispered back. "Just make sure you lock your door and you can text me if you need to. Come on, I'll walk you up there and make sure your door is locked."

I rolled my eyes at Chelsea. She loved to play the desperate card and she did it well, but it wasn't seeming to work this time. Score one for me, even if I was still mad at Clark. Honestly, if there hadn't been a murder tonight, I would have been furious with both of them, but right now I just couldn't expend that much mental energy to the dating situation so I was choosing to ignore it and focus on figuring out who had killed Jake.

Soon enough, the living room was almost empty. Mandy, Tank, my father and I were the only ones left. My father started to bank the fire in the fireplace while Mandy started to blow out the candles in the entryway. I walked over to the window hoping to see some improvement in the storm, but the wind was still blowing the snow around so hard and fast that it looked like someone had hung a painted backdrop outside of our windows. There was no sign of the bird feeders or any of the trees that surrounded our house.

The only thing worse than being stuck out there was being stuck in here, not knowing who the killer was and if they would strike again.

•Chapter Twelve•

As the light in the living room was slowly extinguished, I took out my flip phone and dialed Max's number. I crossed my fingers that the call would go through and was pleasantly surprised when it started to ring. After a few rings, Max picked up.

"Hello Sweet Thing," Max said. "Everyone okay over there?"

"Well besides the dead person and the fact that this entire thing keeps getting more and more complicated, yeah I guess we are okay," I said.

"Sorry Tessa," Max said. He really did sound sorry. "I'm just going a little crazy being stuck at my house and not able to help anyone, especially you. I may have already tried to come help you and gotten my car stuck."

"You didn't," I couldn't help but squeal. At least one of my boyfriends had my back.

"I did," Max said with a chuckle. "I can't actually see it, but my car is stuck at the end of my driveway right now."

I laughed and it felt good to not worry for just a moment. After I was done with my moment of lightness, I filled Max in on everything we had learned so far. I told him the people we had ruled out and the people who had actually touched dinner and the plates that were brought out. And I told him what we had learned about Anna and her boyfriend and Dawn being previously married to Jake.

"Wow, you weren't kidding about it getting more complicated," Max said with a whistle. "I can call the dispatchers again and see if they have anyone headed your way yet."

"Would you?" I asked. "Because I'm a little afraid that whoever did this may get upset if we start to figure it out. You have to admit, the way they killed Jake was pretty clever and I'm sure they think they'll get away with it, so me snooping around isn't going to help."

"Let me try to give them a call and I will get back to you," Max said. "Unfortunately the weather radio I've been listening to says that this storm isn't going anywhere. It has basically parked itself on top of us and isn't moving on."

"Thanks Max," I said.

"And before I go, I'm going to try this again," Max said with a nervous chuckle. "I love you Tessa."

I couldn't help but smile so big that my cheeks felt like they were going to crack. It was almost involuntary.

"I love you too Max," I said, ignoring the goo-goo eyes Mandy was making at me from across the room. "Goodbye."

I gently closed the phone and slid it back into the back pocket of my jeans. What did this all mean? I feel like I had gone from casually dating two guys to all of a sudden being exclusive with one. I didn't really know how I was feeling, but my head was spinning and I knew I couldn't think about it right now because someone in this bed and breakfast had killed Jake and I needed to figure out who it was before anything else could happen.

"So, I couldn't help but overhear," Mandy said as she sidled up to my elbow. "Was that a giant step forward that you and Max just took in your relationship?"

"Yes it was, but no I don't want to talk about it," I said before she could even open her mouth. I couldn't blame her because Mandy had been my best friend before Max and I had even started dating so she had been through all of our previous relationship with me. She knew everything about it and I knew she had been rooting for us to be officially back together for a while.

"That's fine," Mandy said with a sly smile. "But you know where to find me when you want to talk about it. Mostly because I'll be sleeping in the bed next to you because of this stupid storm."

I laughed and gave her a shove. It was nice to have someone who was even closer than a sister to talk to. And I definitely would talk through this entire confusing dating relationship thing with her, just not right now.

"Let's head upstairs," I said, grabbing my flashlight. "I'd like to try to get a little sleep if I could."

Mandy grabbed her flashlight and spun slowly around to make sure there were no candles left burning in the living room. In the entryway, we were joined by Tank and my father who had finished extinguishing all of the candles out there and together the four of us made our way up the stairs.

The hallway that lead to the six guest rooms was eerily quiet. I knew everyone was probably in their rooms talking about exactly the same thing, but no one wanted to draw attention to their rooms. We walked down to the door that separated the guest hallway from our private, family space and stepped through to our cozy little part of the world.

The living room was bathed in light from a camping lantern that my mother had put on the coffee table. Clark was sitting awkwardly on the couch with my mother who was busy knitting something or other. She had just taken up the hobby of knitting, but so far she could only make uneven scarves that for some reason were always in wild colors. The one she was working on now was orange and green and I briefly wondered if she had gone color blind.

"Come on Clark," Tank said gruffly. "You are staying in my room on the fold out sofa."

Tank marched off to his room, not waiting for Clark. Clark glanced at me and I quickly looked away, not wanting to show him how hurt I was. He jumped off of the couch and started off after Tank.

"Girls, you should get to bed," my father said. "I might stay up just a little while longer."

I wanted to stay up with him, but Mandy looped her arm through mine and pulled me off to my bedroom. Once inside, I threw a pair of pajama pants and a t-shirt at

Mandy and we both got dressed. As I was tying my pajama pants, my phone buzzed on the nightstand.

Bad news. Police are still swamped and keep getting police cars stuck in the snow. They've told me they will try to come soon, but probably won't make it to the B&B until morning at the earliest.

I sighed, knowing it wasn't Max's fault. If he couldn't pull any strings, it really must be a really bad situation out there. I sent him a quick message back.

Thank you for trying.

Mandy looked confused, so I handed her my phone. She read the message and handed it back.

"That's not good," she said. "But I know they must be trying."

We climbed into bed and as uncomfortable as it was trying to share a twin sized bed with another person, I was kind of glad I was. It was so cold outside and it was starting to seep into the old house. The furnace hadn't been running for a few hours now and so there was nothing to try to keep the cold air out.

This wasn't the first time we had shared a twin bed. Mandy used to come visit me when I was in college and she needed a weekend away from small town drama. When I lived in the dorms, we had even shared a lofted twin bed, which had been quite the experience. But having Mandy there next to me had been a nice reminder of home when I was far away.

"Tessa," Mandy said, her voice quiet in the still darkness. "Do you really think we are in danger?"

"I'm not sure," I said. "But I do know that whoever did this probably didn't think someone would figure out that it wasn't an accident. And now that we have told everyone that we think it was murder, they might come after us."

I could hear her swallow and take an unsteady breath. I hadn't meant to scare her, but I also didn't want to lie to her. Mandy wasn't dumb. She had probably realized the potential for danger once we started all of this investigating.

"It's okay," I said. "I locked my bedroom door."

"Like that plywood door would keep out a determined killer?" Mandy said with a giggle.

She started laughing harder, which made me laugh too. Soon we had dissolved in girlish giggles, the likes of which hadn't hit us since we had been actual girls, probably having a slumber party just like this one. Every time we thought the giggle fit was over, one of us would start up again until finally a knock came on the door.

"Girls, it's been over a decade since I've had to do this," my mother's voice came through. "But despite the fact that you are full-fledged adults, I'm here to tell you that you need to go to sleep."

All three of us had a good laugh and finally Mandy and I were able to settle down. Mandy's breath started to get slower and more even and I knew she had fallen asleep.

But as I lay there in the dark, I just couldn't get to sleep. I kept running through all of the things I knew about the case in my head and tried to fit the pieces together. So far, it was like trying to do a puzzle where you only had the edge pieces. I could see that everything was going to go together, but I had no idea what joined them up in the middle.

•Chapter Thirteen•

At some point I must have fallen asleep because I was awakened by a knock on my bedroom door. I grabbed my phone off of my nightstand and it said that it was 2:14 in the morning. I sat up straight in bed and Mandy rolled over to face me, her eyes wide.

"Who could that be?" she whispered through her teeth at me.

I shrugged but even in my half-asleep state I figured that if it was the killer, he or she wouldn't have bothered to knock on the door.

The two flashlights were sitting on the nightstand and I gave one to Mandy as I stood up out of bed. We both hit the rubber buttons to turn on the flashlights and I crept to the door. Mandy focused her beam of light on the doorknob.

"Who's there?" I asked quietly.

"It's Dawn," came a voice. "Please let me in. I'm starting to get freaked out."

I looked back at Mandy who simply nodded her head. If Dawn had come here to attack us or something, she would have a hard time getting both of us without us putting up a fight. I unlocked the door and opened it up just wide enough for Dawn to sneak in.

"Sit down," I said firmly as I pulled my desk chair out.

She listened and plopped herself down. I walked backwards until I sat down on the bed. Dawn didn't seem like she was here for anything bad but I didn't want to turn my back on her. Mandy scooted herself over until she was sitting next to me on the edge of the bed.

"You said to tell you if I thought of anything that might be relevant," Dawn said. "And I couldn't sleep tonight, so I was thinking over everything and I realized that something that was common knowledge for me is something that I don't think you are aware of at all."

I glanced at Mandy as I tried to wake up a little more and figure out what Dawn was saying. There was something she knew that we didn't, but she was taking an awfully long time to get to the point.

"Okay, well tell us then," Mandy said impatiently. Mandy didn't like when people beat around the bush. She was much happier when they would be straight to the point and stick to the facts.

"Well, you know Lyle?" Dawn asked, like we would say we didn't. Mandy scowled at her until she continued talking. "Lyle is actually Jake's father."

The world froze around me as once again Dawn dropped this fact on us like a bomb. I wondered how many other secrets she knew that she was still keeping from us. Lyle was Jake's father? We knew why Dawn was here, but why was Lyle here during Jake's honeymoon?

"Did Jake know that?" I asked, realizing immediately that my sleep-addled mind should have thought before it let the words come tumbling out of my mouth. Obviously if Dawn knew, she would have found that out from Jake himself, probably when they were married.

"Yes," Dawn said slowly, giving me an odd look. I kept my straight face, hoping to trick her into thinking I had a line of questioning in mind after that. "But I don't think Anna knew that. At least, she didn't appear to know Lyle at all."

"Were Jake and Lyle on good terms?" I asked.

"Not really, at least they weren't when we were married," Dawn said. "Jake was a rising star and Lyle was desperate to hold

111

on and ride his coattails. Lyle was always bugging Jake to fire his manager and let Lyle take over even though he had absolutely no idea what he was doing. After a while, Jake cut off all contact with him."

I let that soak in for a moment. Mandy was staring out the window, taking it in also. Dawn had a smug look on her face, seeming very proud that she had dropped this important information on us. She just kept smiling as I tried to collect my thoughts.

"I just thought you should know," she finally said. She stood up from the desk chair and grabbed her flashlight as she headed towards the door.

"Wait a minute, how did you get in here?" I asked. I was almost positive my father said he was going to lock the door between the B&B and our family area.

"Oh, about that," Dawn said, shuffling her feet. I could see her cheeks flushing red even in the darkness of my bedroom. "I sort of picked the lock."

"What? Why?" Mandy screeched from beside me before slapping her hand over her mouth.

"I just thought you'd want to know about this right away," Dawn said. "And I knew that I wouldn't be able to get to sleep until I told you."

"Okay, I'll follow you out and re-lock the door," I said.

Dawn stood up and left the room. I grabbed my flashlight and followed her, feeling annoyed about the entire situation. The information was, of course, very valuable but she did not have to pick the lock to bang on my door in the middle of the night with it.

She seemed to almost be floating. I guess telling us that information made her feel lighter. Hopefully she'd be able to sleep now instead of waking people up in the early morning. Dawn turned to give me a smile as she was passing through the living room, but I just couldn't bring myself to return it.

I held the door open between the B&B and our family area. Dawn stepped through and turned back towards me. She still had a smile plastered on her face and in my tired stupor, I kind of wanted to slap it off.

"Go to your room," I said. "I'll stand here until I see you get inside."

"Good night," she tittered.

I simply grunted in return, too annoyed to wish her good night. She floated down the hallway and let herself into her room with a little wave back towards me.

As soon as her door closed, I shut the door and locked it again. I halfway thought about shoving a chair under the doorknob, but I didn't think it would be necessary. Would there really be a second person who would try to pick the lock tonight?

Back in my room, Mandy was still awake, but just barely. She was sitting up against some pillows, waiting for me to return and as I came in, her eyes were just shutting before she jerked awake.

"Tessa," she said, startled by my sudden appearance. "I'm so glad you are back. I just couldn't go back to sleep until I knew you were back here and safe."

"You can go to sleep Mandy," I said. "We can talk more in the morning."

Mandy nodded and pushed her pillow back down so that it was flat on the bed. As soon as her head hit the pillow, she was completely out. I have to admit that I was a little bit jealous because I don't think I'll be able to sleep much at all tonight.

I went through the suspect list in my head, trying to quickly put some pieces in place so that I could get myself to sleep. The least likely was my father, who was only still on the list because we didn't know exactly what was put in Jake's dinner and therefore we couldn't rule him out.

Next I had the two women in Jake's life: Anna and Dawn. Anna had a boyfriend back home that she says Jake knew about and approved of, but we can't prove that. Dawn was married to Jake before and came as a surprise to talk to him about their divorce settlement.

The last suspect was Lyle. Before, I had him as a suspect simply because he had carried out some dinner plates, but now I knew he was Jake's estranged father. It wasn't a motive, but it was a relationship that meant a motive could easily come out of it.

As I sat and thought about the suspects, I looked out the window. Normally, I loved to watch the moon outside, but tonight the storm was still raging on and the moon was completely covered by clouds. It was trying hard to glow through the snow storm but couldn't quite break through.

Moving back home was a different experience, especially because it meant moving into a tiny library room and not my former bedroom. But I felt generally safe here, even though I had once been attacked here. I was surrounded by family and even the small size of my tiny room felt cozy, not restricting. After the attack, the sense of safety had come back without much delay.

But tonight I felt like I was on edge. Dawn's middle of the night appearance had rocked my sense of safety, even though she hadn't come to do anything bad. Knowing that someone could make their way through some of our defenses like the door from the B&B was scary because at this point we didn't know who the killer was and there was no escaping it.

I sat up in bed and the feelings about Peter that I had pushed down before were pushing on the door of my mind. This time, I let them in and as the tears started to quietly flow, my fear was pushed out and replaced by bittersweet memories of Peter.

•Chapter Fourteen•

I did manage to fall asleep eventually, hoping to wake up to a sunrise. Instead, I woke up to more whipping wind and snow. One glance at my alarm clock told me that the power was still out. Mandy woke up as I groaned over the lack of electricity and the need for coffee.

We both got up and quickly got dressed in the freezing cold morning. The furnace had now been off for a while so the entire house was rapidly cooling down. Both Mandy and I layered ourselves up with sweatshirts and wool socks and we headed downstairs.

My parents were already in the kitchen cooking breakfast. Thankfully our old house had a gas stove, so we were still able to cook up a breakfast to warm us up. They also had a kettle of water going to make a large pot of coffee in an old metal coffee urn we didn't bring out often.

We moved into the living room and I was glad to see that there was already a fire roaring in the fireplace. Anna and Claudia were both sitting on opposite ends of the sofa with a book and Cheryl, Linda, Joe, and Dave were working on a puzzle at the table in the corner.

After a polite wave to everyone, I quickly exited to the hallway, trying to decide on my strategy for solving this murder. The only idea I could come up with was to do a more thorough investigation. After we ate breakfast, I decided I would announce that I would be searching each room. I could get Tank to guard everyone in the living room while Mandy and I did a quick walk-through of all of the bedrooms.

As I tried to figure out how to introduce that idea to everyone, Mandy came out into the hallway with a steaming cup of coffee. She was chomping on a piece of gum that she had probably sniffed out like a hunting dog. That girl could find a piece of gum in a haystack.

"Here you go Non-Sleeping Beauty," she said with a sly smile. I wasn't sure how she knew I hadn't slept since she had snored away with no problem. I caught a glimpse in the mirror in the entryway and realized that I had giant bags under my eyes that gave away my restless night.

I moved over to the set of chairs next to the bay window and Mandy followed my lead. I set my coffee cup on the little table and pulled out two blankets from a basket between the chairs, tossing one to Mandy. One way my parents had made the B&B extra cozy was by having blankets everywhere. Anytime they went past a basket of fleece blankets on sale at the store, they would pick through and find any that would fit with the colors and patterns of the B&B. They were comfortable and easy to wash after they've been used.

Mandy's blanket was a very light pink and I looked over to see her all wrapped up looking like a little fluffy, pink cloud. I wrapped mine around my shoulders and then wrapped my hands around my hot cup of coffee.

"So what do you think about what happened last night?" Mandy said quietly before taking a sip of her coffee.

"I think it really makes Lyle into a bigger suspect," I said. "I mean, we have four suspects and now three of them have close relationships and suspicious circumstances. Anna has a boyfriend, Dawn wanted more money, and Lyle and Jake were estranged. It has just complicated things more."

"You're right," Mandy said. "It was helpful and also extremely complicating all at once. So what is our next step?"

"I think we need to search for more clues," I said. "I was just thinking that after breakfast, you and I should go search the guest rooms while Tank guards everyone to make sure no one tries to hide any clues."

Mandy sucked her breath in through her teeth as she scowled. I took a sip of the liquid energy in my cup, understanding what she meant without her having to explain. It would be a hard sell to some of the guests, but it was the necessary next step.

I should also try to get in contact with Max again. Obviously, the police or ambulance hadn't been able to make it here yet and I was starting to understand that we may be on our own for a while here. I needed to step up my investigation game because the police weren't going to be able to help me.

We sat together looking out at the blowing snow while I drained my coffee cup. Mandy sipped hers slowly, trying not to give me a discouraging look. She was always a bit aghast at my eating habits and that included my bottomless appetite for coffee.

Once both of our cups were empty, I figured breakfast must be almost done.

Mandy and I popped into the kitchen just in time to see my dad scooping a final load of bacon onto a serving plate.

"Oh thank goodness," he said. "I need your help to get breakfast on the table. Mandy, can you start bringing out food? And Tessa, could you run upstairs and get the rest of the guests to come down?"

Mandy grabbed a bowl of scrambled eggs and pushed back through the swinging door and I followed close behind. I walked through the dining room and dashed up the stairs, trying to remember who was up and who must still be sleeping. As I got to the top, I figured I may as well start knocking on all of the doors.

I put my hand up to knock on the first door and as I started to hit the door, it swung open suddenly and I just about fell right into a very surprised Dawn. Her eyes were open wide and she jumped back a bit. After regaining my composure, I remembered why I was there.

"Good morning," I said. "It is time for breakfast. Maybe you could help me wake everyone up?"

"Umm, sure," Dawn said, a smile curling up onto her face. "I'll start down at that end with Lyle's room."

I nodded and scooted my way down to the other end. As I knocked on the next door, I quickly realized that I was knocking on Chelsea's door. My lack of sleep did not want to deal with her, but I couldn't do anything about that now.

The door slowly opened and a bleary eyed Chelsea peeked through the slit. Her red hair was sticking up in all directions and she was still in pajamas. When she saw that I was standing there staring at her, she rubbed her eyes a few times as if she might still be sleeping.

"It's time for breakfast," I said. "Get dressed and come downstairs before the food gets cold."

Chelsea simply scowled at me and slammed the door shut again. I sneered at the shut door and moved on. I did remember that the other two rooms down this way were taken by Cheryl and Joe, and Linda and Dave. They were already downstairs, so I moved down to the other end of the hallway where I realized that Dawn was nowhere to be found. As I moved to the end, the last door opened up and Lyle gruffly pushed Dawn out into the hallway.

"You saw my room, now get out," Lyle

was snarling.

"I just wanted to see how your room was different," Dawn said with a shrug. "You let me in so I thought it was okay."

"I didn't really let you in," Lyle said. He shut his door behind him and quickly locked it. "You knocked and I thought it was Claudia. We've been keeping the door locked and I figured she was knocking for me to let her in. I shouted that it was open and you just barged right in."

"Well I'm out now," Dawn said. She was standing with her arms crossed, her chest puffed out proudly.

I stood and looked between the two of them. Lyle was obviously upset, but I couldn't read Dawn's expression. It seemed to be a cross between amusement and satisfaction. The tension seemed to be getting thicker, so I quickly cut through it.

"Breakfast is ready," I said. "Why don't you two head downstairs and I'll go get Tank and Clark."

Lyle barely even acknowledged me before he strode past me down the hallway, leaving Dawn behind. She shrugged at me, as if she wasn't sure what Lyle's problem was. Then she followed him down the stairs.

I didn't want to deal with Clark, so I simply stuck my head through the doorway into our family area and gave a shout.

"Clark, Tank, wake up," I yelled. "Time for breakfast."

After a moment, a sleepy groan came drifting down the hallway into our living room.

"Okay," Tank said. "We will get up."

I was satisfied with that so I headed back down the stairs. Mandy had almost finished setting the table, so I helped her carry the last few things in. Once the table was set, I sat down. The exhaustion was hitting me hard now and I was glad when Mandy came back with another cup of coffee for me.

The guests slowly filtered in and sat down as I tried not to gulp down the hot liquid that was sustaining me. The downside was that I don't think I would be able to take a nap because I won't be able to sleep well until I know I am not stuck here with a killer. Hopefully searching the rooms would bring some clarity to this investigation and answer some questions. Until then, I will just be trying not to fall asleep in my breakfast.

•Chapter Fifteen•

Eventually everyone had made an appearance at the breakfast table and we quietly ate. It was funny looking around at everyone. It was getting colder in the house, so everyone was bundled up but instead it looked like everyone had gained a good ten pounds since the night before because of all the extra layers.

Once breakfast was done, I nodded at Tank. When he had come down to breakfast, I had quickly whispered my plan to him and he agreed to once again stand guard. Tank stood up and stationed himself in the doorway.

"Excuse me," I said, standing up from my chair. "Could I have your attention? Unfortunately, the police are still not here and we need to move on with the investigation. Mandy and I will be doing a quick walk-through of each guest room just to check for anything that might point to a suspect. We will be very careful with your personal items."

A murmur started going around the table and as I glanced around, I saw that Lyle's face was once again turning from pink to red. I was getting the idea that he had a bit of an anger problem and maybe that was part of his estrangement from Jake.

"We ask that you all stay here while we investigate so that we know that nothing has been moved or hidden," I said. "Tank will be here to make sure everyone stays here. We will go quickly, but until we are back, I'm sure my parents will provide you with refills on coffee and orange juice and perhaps some trays of cookies or some other goodies."

Lyle stood up so violently that his chair tipped over backwards. He slammed the palms of his hands onto the table as his anger almost seemed to shoot out of his ears. Everyone jumped and turned to face him.

"How dare you trap us here," Lyle shouted. "You are not the police and you have no right to do this."

I tried my hardest to remain calm and to keep my face in an even expression. As I tried to decide how to respond, Dave stood up from his spot across the table from Lyle and leaned forward towards Lyle.

"Do you have something to hide?" Dave asked. "If you don't, you wouldn't be so angry I suppose. I would assume that anyone who didn't kill Jake would be eager to have their own name cleared and to figure out who actually did it. I think you need to sit back down and let these women try to solve this mystery."

For a moment, the two men stood and stared at each other. Lyle's face slowly drained until it was back to being a very annoyed shade of pink. He slowly sat down and once he was in his chair, Dave sat back down and nodded at me.

"I promise we will be fast," I said. "Thank you for your cooperation."

Mandy and I quickly slid past Tank and dashed up the stairs, not wanting to stay in the dining room longer than we had to. I took the lead and together we walked to the end of the hallway. We decided to start on the end with Chelsea's room because she wasn't a suspect.

We did a quick walk-through of Chelsea's room, finding nothing of interest. I was actually a little disappointed that I didn't find anything embarrassing to use against her, but that was just my pettiness flaring up.

The next two rooms belonged to Linda and Dave, and Cheryl and Joe. We did a quick walk-through of each one and as expected, found nothing of interest. As we moved on, I started to feel a little sick to my stomach. What if we didn't find anything and we were back where we started except now we have invaded everyone's privacy? Even worse, what if we did find something? I suppose we would just have to deal with whatever happened and move on from there.

Dawn's room was next and as we walked in, I noticed how neat and tidy everything was. Normally, people on vacation were a bit cluttered. They would leave their suitcases open with clothes spilling out or pile up the little coffee table with magazines and snacks. One of the best parts of going on vacation was being able to be a bit untidy because other people would take care of it.

But this room was spotless. Either Dawn was hiding something or she was a neat freak. Mandy opened up the lid of her suitcase to find it empty. I opened the dresser drawers to find them lovingly stacked with piles of neatly folded clothing. One drawer had underthings while another held shirts and the last one held pants. Mandy opened the nightstand drawer and turned to shrug at me, apparently finding nothing of note.

Together we walked into the little bathroom and marveled at how neat it all was. A toothbrush and a hairbrush sat next to the sink alongside a little toiletry bag. We poked the bag open to find everything neatly arranged inside. Even the shower was neatly stocked with travel bottles of shampoo and conditioner and a washcloth.

Mandy and I walked out of the bathroom and stood in the bedroom together. I slowly turned around, looking for something, anything out of place.

"Don't you think it's all a bit too neat?" Mandy asked quietly.

"Yes, I really do," I said. "I don't think I've ever seen a guest room so neat unless there isn't actually anyone staying in it."

"Do you think she is hiding something?" Mandy asked.

"I'm really not sure," I said. "If she is, she has hidden it quite well."

"We should go to the next room," Mandy said. "We said we would be quick so we need to keep moving."

As she started towards the door, I turned around slowly once more time, looking for anything that stuck out to me, but nothing jumped. Reluctantly, I followed Mandy out and locked the door behind us.

The next room was the honeymoon suite. We called it that, but only about two nights a month was it actually used by a honeymooning couple. Having a newlywed couple staying here for a week was different. This room was the biggest room and had a large bathroom with a big, whirlpool tub.

As we walked in, an air of sadness settled over me. One glance at the bed made tears spring to my eyes. The bed was rumpled but on one side was a pile of clothing. Anna had taken Jake's clothing and piled it onto the bed to sleep next to. I assumed that it was something to trick her in the middle of the night and convince her that maybe he was still right there next to her.

After Peter died, I had saved all of his dirty clothing from the laundry basket and one by one, I would sleep with a piece next to me in the bed. Once it didn't smell like him anymore, I would get another piece. I was able to fool myself with the smell of him for a while. A few months later I woke up in the middle of the night and realized that I couldn't smell him anymore and there weren't any more pieces of dirty clothing left. I cried for hours until I was all out of tears and I had cried myself into a headache.

As I stood in the middle of the room and cried, Mandy took the initiative to search the room. The realization hit me that I couldn't remember what Peter smelled like. I could remember his cologne, but not his natural smell and now I would never be able to smell it again.

I grabbed a tissue off of the nightstand and tried my hardest to pull myself together. Once I was able to gulp back the rest of my tears, Mandy took me by the elbow and moved me gently towards the door. She brought me into the hallway and took my keys to lock the door behind me. Then she wrapped me in a large hug.

"Let me know if you need to talk," she said.

"You didn't find anything?" I asked with a sniffle.

"Nothing out of the ordinary," Mandy said. "I'm sorry I didn't have you wait in the hallway to save you from that."

"Mandy, I hope you never have to experience grief like this," I said as I grabbed her hand and squeezed. "Sometimes it will hit no matter what and you just have to work through it. There was nothing you could do about it. This episode of grief has been coming on for a while now."

"We only have one more room," Mandy said. "Are you up for it?"

I nodded and together we walked to Lyle and Claudia's door. If we didn't find anything in here, we would still have no idea who had killed Jake and we would still be stuck in the B&B with a dead body and a killer until the storm subsided and the police were able to make it here.

Mandy pushed the door open and with a glance back at me, she stepped through the doorway. That glance told me that she was thinking the same thing. It wasn't that we wanted to find something in this specific room, but we wanted to find something, somewhere.

The room was quite tidy and I had a feeling that Lyle was a bit fussy about things like that. Mandy headed to the bedroom while I started with the nightstands. There were phone chargers and a paperback book; nothing out of the ordinary.

I moved over to the small sitting area and searched around for anything that didn't belong in the room. As far as I could see, everything was in place. Mandy walked out of the bathroom, shaking her head.

"I don't see anything in there," she said.

I sighed as I plopped myself down on to the love seat. This was the last guest room and had been the last hope to find a clue to solve this murder. I wasn't really sure where we should go from here. My worst fear at the moment was that this blizzard would and everyone would leave, never knowing who had murdered Jake.

Leaning back, something behind a pillow stuck into my back. What in the world was hiding in this couch? I leaned forward and pulled the pillow off of the couch, tossing it onto the ground.

Sitting wedged halfway into seam of the couch was a small bottle. Something clicked inside of me and a small ray of hope started to shine inside of me. I grabbed a tissue out of a box on the table and used it to pick up the bottle.

In large letters on the front of the small bottle, it said FISH SAUCE. I turned slowly to look at Mandy, holding out the bottle for her to read. As her eyes slowly grew to the size of dinner plates, I could feel a smile growing on my face. We finally had something to help us solve this murder.

•Chapter Sixteen•

"That isn't mine," Lyle insisted, pounding his fists on the dining room table. "I have no idea how that made it's way into our room, but I didn't put it there."

Tank rolled his eyes from where he stood cross-armed next to the door. It was our way of putting Lyle into a citizen's arrest until the police came to get him.

"Well it either came from you or Claudia," I said. "And I don't think Claudia even knows about Jake, right? You were hoping to mend your relationship with Jake before telling Claudia that you had not only a son, but a famous son."

Lyle's face was red and I was slightly afraid he was going to have a heart attack as he glared at us from the table. Instead, he stood up from his chair and pointed his finger at me.

"Claudia doesn't know and you better not tell her," he said.

"Or what, you'll poison me too?" I asked. "Unfortunately, I don't have any allergies for you to take advantage of Lyle."

For a moment, I thought for sure that Lyle was going to explode. His chest puffed up

and his rage seemed to fill him up. Tank
took a few steps towards Lyle and stared at
Lyle until their eyes met.

"If I were you, I'd sit back down," Tank
growled.

Lyle looked Tank up and down before he
realized that even though he was a big man,
Tank was bigger. Wisely, he chose to sit
back down in his chair. He deflated, looking
like a much smaller man suddenly.

"I would never use Jake's allergy like
that," Lyle said. "We spent so long when he
was a child protecting him and making sure
he never had to worry about having a
reaction like that. What I watched play out
in the dining room last night was my worst
nightmare come true."

Tears were shining in Lyle's eyes and I
wondered briefly if we were wrong. Maybe
Claudia had done it? That was the only
other way I could think of that the bottle of
fish sauce had ended up hidden in their
room, stuffed behind a couch cushion.

"I think we need to all take a moment to
breathe," I said. "I'm going to get us some
coffee and treats. Lyle, please stay here and
let Mandy know if you need anything. Tank
will stay just to make sure everyone is safe."

I pushed my way through the swinging

door and took a deep breath. With both hands on the counter, I let myself collapse down a little bit. Between my restless night and trying to figure this murder out, I could feel myself wearing down fast.

My phone buzzed in my pocket and I pulled it out, a little bit proud that I actually felt the vibration. For a phone with such a prominent 'mute ringer' button, it sure did a poor job of using the vibrate mode to make up for all of the accidental phone muting. I flipped it open, seeing a message from Max.

Good news, there is a break in the storm. The police should be on their way. I am trying to find a way over also. Stay safe Sweet Thing :) Love you

Max knew just what to say to make me smile. My heart felt like it was melting a bit, even through the fog of exhaustion. And he had good news because the arrival of the police meant we no longer had to deal with a murder suspect and a dead body. I realized I hadn't told him about my discovery, so I typed a quick message back to him.

We are staying safe. We searched the guest rooms and I found a bottle of fish sauce in one room. We are currently detaining the suspect. I hope the police get here fast so that we don't have to deal with it anymore. Love you too :)

The message was delivered, but just after that my phone died. Shoot, I really should get better at plugging my phone in more often. Even though the battery on this phone could last for about five days straight, I realized I hadn't plugged it in for almost a week. And now the power was out, so I couldn't plug it in. Oops.

I piled a plate with some cookies and grabbed mugs and a carafe of coffee. Pushing my way through the door, I set everything with a clunk onto the table in front of Lyle. Before anyone else could serve themselves, I poured a cup of coffee for myself. I was in such a rush for that sweet caffeine that I spilled droplets all over the table. Mandy scowled and walked into the kitchen, reappearing with a rag to wipe up my mishap. I gave her a guilty smile and she rolled her eyes at me with a grin.

"I do have one thing I'd like," Lyle said. "Can you please bring Claudia in here so I can explain what is going on? I mean, I don't know about the bottle of fish sauce, but I want her to hear about Jake from me."

"Sure, I will go to get her," I said.

I strolled out and down the hallway to the living room where everyone was trying to busy themselves. I avoided looking at Clark, who was reading a book on the sofa. Chelsea was sitting next to him, looking like she was trying her hardest to cuddle up him as much as she possibly could. When she saw me, she practically jumped into his lap, but Clark shifted himself so that she was forced to retreat.

Claudia was sitting in an armchair with my mother next to her, trying to make polite conversation to distract her from the fact that Lyle had been forced to leave the living room. When Claudia noticed that I had walked in, she stood up, letting the blanket in her lap slip down to the floor. She stared at me for a moment before I beckoned her to follow me. Slowly, she walked into the hallway behind me.

"What is going on Tessa?" she asked.

"Lyle said he would like to explain things to you," I said, turning and leading her into the dining room.

The room was bathed in candlelight and the soft glow of the camping lantern. When Lyle saw Claudia, he stood up and she rushed towards him, collapsing into his arms with a quiet cry. For a moment, they both seemed to lean on each other for support. It was such an intimate moment that I actually looked away, feeling like a creep for watching them in their time of need.

"Lyle, what is going on?" Claudia finally asked as she pulled back from his embrace.

Lyle helped Claudia into a chair before he sat back down in his spot before telling her everything about Jake. Claudia's face grew from confusion to horror as she realized the weight of what Lyle was saying. Not only did he have a son that he hadn't told her about, but the weekend he was going to introduce them, his son had died.

"So Jake was your son," Claudia said slowly. "I understand that, but why are they making you stay here in the dining room?"

"Well that is the part I can't really explain," Lyle said. A few tears were falling down his face now and Claudia reached forward and gently brushed them away.

"Claudia, I can explain that part," I said, feeling a little sorry for Lyle before I remembered that he was a murderer. "When we searched the guest rooms, your room was the only room where we found a clue. We found a bottle of fish sauce in the couch cushions. Unfortunately, between that and the fact that Jake and Lyle were estranged, everything is pointing to the fact that Lyle was the one who did it."

A gut-wrenching wail escaped Claudia's lips and she collapsed back into her chair, covering her face with her hands. Lyle leaned forward to comfort her before pulling back, unsure if that was what she wanted. After a moment, he put his hand lightly on her knee.

"That can't be right," Claudia said as she lowered her hands. "Lyle couldn't have done it. I know how it looks, but it just can't be right. My Lyle would never do that to someone, especially someone he loved like Jake."

"But why were they estranged then?" I asked. I felt like a terrible human being for questioning someone's love for their own child, but someone had to ask.

"We were estranged because I made some dumb decisions once," Lyle said. "When Jake was just starting out in show business, we still had a good relationship. That was over a decade ago and I moved to California to help give him some guidance. But then I got greedy."

Lyle was fidgeting with his wedding ring as he talked, spinning it around and around his finger. He stared at his hands and avoided eye contact with any of us, especially Claudia. We all stayed quiet waiting for him to continue talking.

"Instead of giving him paternal advice, I started to only focus on the money," Lyle said, his voice catching in his throat slightly. A tear trickled down his cheek as he talked. "We were living the good life and I was pushing him to work harder, take on more work, do more commercials even though he hated them. All I saw were dollar signs."

Claudia sniffled and Mandy handed her a tissue. Even Tank's angrily crossed arms had relaxed a bit as he listened.

"And then one day, Jake had had enough," Lyle continued. "He went out and found a real agent and asked me to leave. I fought against it, even bringing him to court over money I thought he owed me. But eventually I listened and moved back to Minnesota even though I still thought he was a terrible son for cutting off his own father. But then I met Claudia."

Lyle leaned forward and gently took both of Claudia's hands in his own. She stared at her lap for a moment before raising her eyes to meet his.

"Claudia is the love of my life," he said, gazing into her eyes. "She loves me no matter how much of a jerk I am and she helped me change. She made me see my shortcomings and work on them. And here I am a better man."

Claudia raised their hands to her lips and kissed Lyle's hands gently. He smiled, a look of relief passing through his face. The rest of us sat spellbound, listening for Lyle to finish his story.

"And then Jake got married and I wasn't invited," he said. "I was heartbroken and determined to patch things up. Jake's mother told me that he would be here for his honeymoon and as soon as I heard, I called and booked us a room. I figured I would be able to talk to him and patch things up before we introduced our wives to each other."

"That would have been beautiful," Claudia said, almost in a whisper.

"But Hollywood had changed Jake and he wasn't willing to forgive you, was he?" I chimed in. We needed to get to the end of this story.

"It certainly did," Lyle said with a nod. "He would hardly give me the time of day. He told me in no uncertain terms that there was no way he would even talk to me. Jake told me to stay away from his wife and that he didn't want to meet my wife either. I was very upset, but later on, I got the impression that he was softening. Even though he was a little grumpy, he let me make polite conversation with him and he even caught my eye and smiled a few times. I was so hopeful that it was a good sign until he collapsed at dinner."

Lyle's heavy story hung in the air; the emotions in the room were weighing everything down. I needed to escape it before I burst. My fatigued mind was still full of the emotions that had been brought up over remembering Peter's death. I needed to get out of this room.

"Thank you Lyle," I said. "I would ask that you simply stay here in this room until the police come."

Lyle started to protest, but I burst through the swinging door to the kitchen, gulping in air as if I had just burst out of the depths of the sea. I sank into one of the chairs and folded my arms on the kitchen table, lowering my head as I started to sob.

As much as I wanted to run through Lyle's story and look for more clues, I just couldn't right now. Instead, I sobbed into my shirt sleeves until they were wet, letting memories of Peter flow through my mind.

•Chapter Seventeen•

"Tessa, are you alright?"

Someone had their hand on my shoulder, shaking me awake. Crying away my emotions had been exhausting and at some point I had dozed off. I sat up and rubbed my eyes. The snow was still blowing like crazy outside, which made it hard to know what time it was or how long I had been sleeping. I had to imagine it wasn't long since I was in the kitchen.

I glanced up and saw that Clark had been the one to shake me awake. Great, as if I wasn't upset enough, let's add that the man I've been seeing who kissed another girl in my house. I really didn't want to deal with this situation right now, but we were both stuck in this house until the storm was gone.

"Are you alright?" Clark asked again.

"No," I said. "I mean yes, but no. I don't really want to talk about it."

"You can tell me Tessa," Clark said.

I stood up and looked at his face. Clark was at least a head taller than me, which was both exciting and annoying. His height made him seem like a protector, but it also meant that kissing was an interesting experiment in tip-toe balancing, not that I wanted to think about kissing him right now. He put his hand on my elbow and gazed down into my eyes.

"Please, Tessa, is it about Peter?" he asked quietly.

I pulled back involuntarily, hating the sound of Peter's name coming from his lips. Between the emotional roller coaster I had just sent myself on and the sudden realization that we were standing on the same spot where I had caught him kissing Chelsea, I felt myself fill up with negativity.

"You want to talk about my dead husband?" I snarled. "Maybe we should talk a little bit about you kissing Chelsea. Should we drag all of the other loves of our life into our conversation?"

Clark's eyebrows knit together as he tried to follow my train of thought. As I spoke, I know it didn't make any sense, but my anger was like a runaway train right now and I wasn't sure where it was going to end up. I took another step back from him. I didn't want to be close enough to smell his cologne and see his cute dimple. The anger was welling up inside and I wanted it to.

"Tessa, you know that Chelsea and I date

just like you and Max do," Clark said. I think if I wasn't filled with anger he would have sounded reasonable, but through my rage glasses he sounded like he was trying to tell me to calm down. And no one tells me to calm down.

"Yeah, but I don't bring him to your house and kiss him in your kitchen," I yelled slamming a chair into the table. "If there wasn't a blizzard raging outside, I would have asked you to leave yesterday. But while I don't hate you enough to want you to get lost in this blizzard, I would like you to stay away from me."

This time it was Clark's turn to take a step back. He almost stumbled like I had given him a shove. I immediately regretted the words that had flown out of my mouth. My absolute worst trait is my inability to shut my mouth. On some level I knew I should just stop talking, but I couldn't. My anger was driving the bus right now.

Clark puffed himself back up and gathered up his courage. His eyes narrowed at me and I could see anger start to flow through him too.

"Tessa, maybe we need to take a break," Clark said. "I'm tired of this. I'm tired of being the one that you go out with for fun. I know you don't want a serious relationship, but I still want you to be able to trust me enough to tell me things. You tell Max about Peter."

"Max understands what I'm going through because he's going through it too," I said. "I've always been afraid I'd drive you away if I talked about all of my feelings about Peter's death and how I still cry and sometimes I dream of him and it seems so real that I wake up thinking he is still sleeping next to me. I didn't want you think I was hung up on Peter, but I'm still dealing with it. And you are the new guy in town. I didn't think you wanted to be saddled with a girl who can't get over her dead husband."

"I'm not saddled with you," Clark said. "Look, I've been putting up with your hidden emotions and your feelings of inadequacy for a few months now. I know I'm seen as some kind of prize in this town. I know I like to flirt and that makes tongues wag around Shady Lake. But I'm not that conceited. I didn't come along and pick you like you were some kind of trophy that I could drag up the social ladder of this town. I'm tired of propping you up all of the time."

I was stunned into silence for a while as

Clark's words echoed in my ears. I'd been struggling with not feeling good enough for Clark for a while now, but I had no idea he could see that struggle.

"I see how you glare at any girl who makes eyes at me when we are out together," Clark continued. "I know you are still nervous every single time we go out together even though we've been dating for over six months now. And I hate that."

"So why didn't you break up with me before this?" I asked.

"Because I was hoping you would change," Clark said quietly. "I was hoping you would relax and start to tell me things. Apparently I hoped too much because you seem to not trust me with your emotional struggles."

"Does this mean you don't think we should date anymore?" I asked, trying to push down the tears that were springing red-hot into my eyes.

"It means that I think we should take a break," he said. "Don't worry, I will make sure Chelsea doesn't rub it in your face."

For a moment, the world swirled around us as we stood toe to toe in the kitchen. I couldn't bring myself to look him in the eyes, knowing that if I did the tears in my eyes would spill over. Clark leaned forward and kissed my forehead, letting his warm lips linger a little longer than he usually would.

Then he turned and walked through the door into the living room, leaving me with even more emotional baggage during this blizzard. I plopped back down into one of the chairs, trying to figure out where to go from here. The kitchen clock was frozen in place and my phone was out of battery, so I had no idea what time it was. I could only hope that the police would get here soon.

I glanced out the window, wondering what Max meant when he said there was a break in the storm. I may have missed it during my little nap, but it looked exactly the same as it had since the storm had blown in yesterday. The wind was still whipping the snow every which way making it so dark outside that it seemed like evening, even though if I had to guess it was probably about lunchtime. I wasn't going to go outside in this, but I knew from experience that this kind of wind blew snow in every direction making it impossible to even know up from down when you were out in it.

Out of the corner of my eye, I could see

the swinging door start to open. Mandy's head poked in. As soon as she saw me, she slipped in and sat in the chair across the table from me. For a moment, she didn't say anything. She gave me the same sympathetic look I'd seen so many times in my life. It was the same one that saw me through failing my driver's test the first time and pre-wedding jitters. It had been there when my freshman year high school crush didn't dance with me at the spring fling and when Peter had died.

After a moment, she reached across the table and held my hand. Whereas my biggest fault was not being able to shut my mouth, one of Mandy's biggest strengths was knowing when to wait out the silence. There we sat, mirror images of each other. We had always been told we looked alike, but sometimes we were opposites. Right now I was the face of grief while Mandy was a pillar of strength.

"Thank you," I finally managed to say. "Clark and I were just talking."

"I know," Mandy said, cutting me off. "I could hear through the door. I didn't think you'd mind me listening in."

Her impish grin made me giggle. It was just enough to drag me out of the depths of depression to a shallower depth of sadness. I actually was glad she had listened in so that I didn't have to rehash the entire conversation for her. Instead, she let me just sit with her and my sadness for a little while.

"Okay, that's enough," she said after a few minutes of wallowing. "It is lunchtime and someone needs to make food. You are going to help me pull together some plates of sandwich fixings for everyone."

I stood up, grateful for her initiative. As we pulled sliced meat and condiments out of the fridge, I watched Mandy work to make the ugly foods look appetizing. I felt so grateful for her and I felt such a deep love, the kind you can only have for a friend that has been through everything life throws your way.

At that moment I knew that no matter what happened with Clark and I, Mandy would always be there for me. As soon as the storm let up and the police came, I could work on getting my life back on track.

•Chapter Eighteen•

The sound of the crackling fire was enough to cover all of the chewing noises from everyone in the living room. We had first brought the trays to Claudia and Lyle, warning Tank to hold off because if he had been at the front of the line no one else would have gotten a sandwich.

I settled myself into a chair in the library corner with my sandwich. It was the only spot in the room that didn't have other seating close to it. I wanted to eat by myself, but it was cold in the kitchen. This was the next best thing right now.

Mandy, however, wouldn't let me be all alone. She took one look at my sad self, marched over and demanded I hold her plate before she moved an ottoman closer to sit on. We didn't even talk, but I had to admit that having her sit next to me did help a little. Especially because it was easier to ignore Chelsea and Clark when I had someone with me.

Once I finished off my lunch, I gathered a few plates to bring into the kitchen. As I set them in the sink, I heard the door open again behind me. I figured Mandy was helping me clean up, but when I turned around I was surprised to see that Anna had followed me in.

"Tessa, may I talk to you?" she said.

"Of course, why don't you sit down?"

We both sat at the kitchen table, which seemed to be the headquarters for my investigation. Anna's eyes were ringed in red and her nose looked raw, probably from wiping it so much. My heart broke for her and her situation.

"I couldn't help but notice that you have Lyle in the other room and he hasn't been allowed back with us," Anna said. "I'd love to talk to him."

"Why?" I asked.

"Because I know that he was Jake's father," she said. "And I feel just terrible that I never really got to talk to him."

Anna stared at me. There was a twinkle in her eye that seemed amused by my confusion. I was almost glad to see it. It told me that after everything was through, she would come out the other side of this stronger.

"I was under the impression that Jake didn't want to repair his relationship with Lyle," I said. I didn't want to give too much away, but every time I thought I had everything figured out, something else was revealed that changed things.

"Well, at first he was upset," Anna said. "He was mostly upset that his father was crashing our honeymoon. But he had already told me about his estranged father and that he thought they had been estranged long enough. He was hoping for an opportunity to try to patch things up, but Lyle's appearance here annoyed him."

I could understand why. I wouldn't want my parents showing up on my honeymoon. Up until now, I figured Lyle's motive for poisoning Jake was to get revenge for not repairing their relationship. But if Jake had told Anna about his father and seemed to be softening his attitude towards Lyle, why would Lyle still go ahead with his plan? It didn't make any sense.

"Thank you for telling me, Anna," I said. "I'll go check with Lyle to see if he'd like to talk to you."

As I pushed my way through the swinging door to the dining room, I ran through everything in my head again. There was something weird about all of this and it wasn't just that all of the motives we found kept getting pulled apart.

"Lyle, Anna was wondering if she could

come in and talk to you," I said.

Lyle's eyes darted up to meet mine and I could see the pain in them. I realized that he probably thought she wanted to confront him as the wife of a murder victim and not as his daughter-in-law. I didn't want to give anything away, but I did want to reassure him a bit.

"Don't worry," I said. "It isn't anything bad."

I couldn't blame Lyle when he looked like he didn't believe me, but Anna pushed her way through the door and sat in a chair across the table from Claudia and Lyle. For a moment, nobody spoke. Anna picked at her fingernails while Claudia watched her in confusion. Lyle's eyes darted all over the room, trying to figure out whether he should look at her or not. Finally, Anna spoke.

"I know you were Jake's father," she said in a quiet voice. "And I know that Jake said he didn't want to repair your relationship, but after he threw that little fit, he thought it over a little more and he told me about you. Jake had decided ten years was long enough to be estranged and he was going to talk to you after dinner that night."

Lyle's face was a mixture of relief and

grief; the two emotions fighting for a prominent position on his face. At that moment, I knew they would be alright. I slipped quietly back through the door to the kitchen. I needed to do some serious thinking.

As I got myself another cup of coffee, I suddenly realized what had really been bugging me about this entire situation. As a lover of everything true crime, I know that it is well documented that poison was a woman's weapon. Men tend to use knives or more violent weapons while women tend to distance themselves by using poison. Having Lyle essentially poison Jake would go entirely against type.

Of course, it was possible for a man to use poison. It was just highly unlikely. All of a sudden, things were stacking up in a way that made Lyle look like he was taking the fall for something he did not do.

Either of the other two suspects would make sense because they were both women; Anna and Dawn had still not been entirely ruled out as suspects. But then how did the bottle of fish sauce end up in Lyle's room? I suppose it could have been planted there, but by who? And when?

Things were just not adding up and I was

running out of ideas of what to do next. Maybe I should just wait for the police to come and push everything over to them. After all, it wasn't my investigation. I wasn't a detective or anything. I was just a busy body who keeps falling into these things.

Mandy came in just at the right time and I borrowed her phone to send Max a message.

Hey Max, Tessa here. Any ETA on those cops?

Max must have been practically sitting on top of his phone because immediately there was a message back.

Bad news. The cops who were dispatched slid into a light pole. They are alright, but unfortunately we are now down another car and two officers, so you will just have to sit tight.

I groaned and almost dropped the phone. Mandy leapt forward with a little yelp and grabbed her smartphone from me, reading the message and adding her groan to my own.

"So we are still stuck with a killer and a dead body?" she squeaked.

"Yes, but that isn't all the bad news," I said. "I'm beginning to think Lyle didn't do it."

"But the fish sauce bottle," Mandy said.

I cut her off and explained everything that I had just been mulling over and when I got to the end, Mandy couldn't help but agree that I may just be right.

"So what do we do now?" she asked.

I appreciated that she thought I would have any idea what to do, but I was as clueless as she was despite my incessant true crime love. We had suspects, but none of them lined up properly. We had found what had probably poisoned Jake, but couldn't prove who had done it. And we had motives, but none of the motives seemed to hold up.

"For now, we go through to the living room and warm up by the fire," I said.

I stood up and took a deep breath before I walked into the living room. I hoped that something would happen soon, but I was afraid that anything that would help me would hurt someone else.

•Chapter Nineteen•

A little while later, I was feeling much better. Mandy had shoved a stack of trashy magazines in my lap as she plopped down onto the ottoman once I was settled in the secluded chair. I had to assume that one of the guests had brought them along, but after paging through a few I had to admit I was feeling a bit more relaxed.

Looking around the living room, everyone was still on edge. The double date couples had started another puzzle and everyone else seemed to be lazily paging through books. They had all stopped even glancing towards the windows as it was still the foggy, snowy gray that had been whipping by for the past day or so.

"Tessa, I'm afraid I have one more thing to ask you," a voice came from beside me, startling me even though it was just barely above a whisper. I turned to see Anna standing there.

"I need your help," Anna said. "I just remembered that yesterday before dinner I had asked Jake to hold onto my ring. He had given me a cocktail ring that I usually wore on my right hand, but it has always been a little big. I didn't want to lose it, so I gave it to him to hold onto last night. But then after everything happened I kind of forgot until now. I'd love if you helped me get it back so that I could wear it again."

I hesitated for a moment. That would be tampering with the body and removing something that could possibly be evidence, at least in my mind. But the logical half was torn with the emotional half because I also understood clinging on to anything I could that would help me remember Peter. I actually sometimes still wore my wedding ring when I was alone in my room. I certainly still wore the other jewelry he had given me while we were together.

"Sure, I can help you get that," I said. "But I would like to take pictures of exactly what you are taking and where it was on him. I don't want to be insensitive, but it could be evidence."

Anna nodded and I stood up. Dawn came rushing over, almost falling over a pillow that someone had placed on the floor. Her face was distressed and I wondered if Anna knew about Dawn and her marriage to Jake yet.

"Did I hear you are going to disturb that poor man's body?" Dawn hissed at us, looking around to see if anyone else heard her. "That is something the police should do, not Mrs. Pretend Private Eye."

"This is not something to concern you," I said firmly. Anna looked liked she was about to cry and I couldn't blame her. It wasn't like she was going to desecrate a corpse; she simply wanted her ring back.

"I don't think you should go onto that porch," Dawn said, moving between us and the doorway.

She was speaking quietly and I'm sure no one could actually hear her, but everyone was still looking at her curiously. Her mousy hair was flying in every direction and her eyes were darting everywhere. After a moment, Clark walked over and gently took her arm, moving her away from us and back towards the chair she had been in.

I gave him a thankful look and he smiled ever so slightly back at me. I filed away his facial expression in my memory to go over later. Despite how angry I had been with him, my heart still jumped when he smiled at me. Was he just being polite or was there still some hope for our relationship? I would have to think that over later. Right now, I was just trying to keep everything together despite all of the twists and turns in this investigation.

Dawn on the other hand looked like she was seething with anger. Why didn't she want us to search Jake's body? Was she the killer perhaps? I ignored Chelsea's exaggerated scowl and grabbed my flashlight from the floor next to the chair.

I held my hand out for Mandy's phone. She slid it into my hand, giving me a questioning look, obviously wondering if she should come along. I shook my head, just slightly. I think now that we were looking for more clues, I would need to make sure we split up more often to cover more ground here in the B&B, at least until the police come along.

As we left the light of the living room, it felt like we were slowly sinking into darkness. The candles had been lit in the hallway again, but their glow gave off more familiarity than light. We only had the one flashlight to guide us down the hallway.

The beam of light showed us only the next few steps as we trudged towards the porch. I was filled with unease, but this time I knew it wasn't just because of the dark. We were moving towards a dead body, someone who shouldn't have died.

And I didn't know who did it.

•Chapter Twenty•

Once Anna and I reached the back porch, I handed my flashlight to her and instructed her to point it straight at the body while I took pictures. Slowly, I pulled the blanket off of Jake's body. It was so cold our here that he seemed almost perfectly preserved. I took a deep breath and started clicking the camera a few times, moving around the body to capture all angles.

"Do you know where it was at?" I asked. I really didn't want to have to dig around in the pockets of a corpse longer than necessary.

"I'm pretty sure he put it in the right chest pocket of his shirt," Anna said. "He dropped it in there and I'm pretty sure he wouldn't have taken it out to switch it anywhere else."

I knelt down and gently patted the pocket of his shirt. There was certainly something in the pocket, but it didn't feel like a ring. It felt flat and smooth instead of bumpy. This couldn't possibly be the ring, but what was it. I reached inside and pulled out a piece of paper. I threw a puzzled look to Anna, who looked just as confused as I felt. I unfolded the paper and read inside.

You thought you were rid of me, but you weren't. Surprise! We aren't divorced yet. I'll sign the papers as soon as you give me more money. If you don't, I'll tell your wife that the two of you aren't actually married. Dawn.

The large, loopy writing looked girlish and childlike. I looked from it to Anna, who stuck out her hand to read it. I handed it over, not knowing how much Anna already knew. Her eyes flicked over the paper a few times as she tried to take everything in.

"You mean, he was married to Dawn?" she said. Her voice came out breathy and full of disbelief. "Jake told me he had been married before, but he didn't say it was to Dawn."

"Well apparently he was still technically married to her," I said before realizing that I sounded like an absolute jerk.

I took the note gently out of Anna's hands, realizing I should take a picture of it for posterity. As I documented it, I read it again. So Dawn had lowered herself to blackmail to pay off her shopping debts.

"I can't believe it," Anna said. She knelt down and gently touched Jake's face. "Poor Jake, this was probably why he's been in such a bad mood while we've been here. I thought it was because of Lyle. But he was trying to figure out this divorce situation."

Jake always seemed to be in a bad mood to me, but I just had to take Anna's word for it that he had been acting out of the ordinary this time. Not only had he been confronted on his honeymoon by his estranged father, but also by his ex-wife who was blackmailing him for more money. I had to admit that I was genuinely touched by Anna's affection for him. She was willing to look past so much and simply see Jake underneath it all.

"Anna, the ring wasn't in that pocket," I said. "Is there anywhere else it could be?"

For a moment, Anna continued to gaze at her dead husband's face. Then she looked up at me, a few tears threatening to spill over.

"If it isn't there, I don't know where it is," she said. "Unless he switched it to a different pocket."

I gently patted his other shirt pocket along with the pockets of his jeans, but they all appeared to be empty. The ring was nowhere to be found and I had to be the one to break the bad news to her.

"I don't feel the ring anywhere," I said.

Anna started to cry, tears dripping down

her cheeks and onto Jake's cold, pale face. I could tell that if I wasn't there, she would be wailing. But she was pushing her grief into a private place and only letting the necessary tears flow. I wanted to reach out and tell her that it was alright, that she could let it out. But she didn't know me and I didn't want to tell her about Peter. This was her time to grieve, not my time to play Number One Widow.

"I'm sorry," I said. "I really did try to look. Maybe it was dropped in the dining room when he collapsed."

"Yes maybe," Anna said, turning to face me. "Thank you Tessa, I know you were trying to find it."

For a moment, we sat and looked at each other. I felt bad for judging her harshly before. I had assumed she was some dumb California girl riding an actor's coattails to success. But here she was, looking more sincere than ever. The shame rose up inside of me as I realized that sometimes it wasn't just my mouth that I couldn't control, but it was also my gut reactions.

"I promise I will find that ring for you," I said. "Could you tell me what it looks like?"

Anna described a ring that sounded gorgeous. It had a beautiful, blue emerald in the middle with a few diamond chips around the outside.

"It wasn't that big or that valuable," she said. "But it meant a lot to me. It was one of the first things Jake gave me."

She giggled to herself as she reached out to grab Jake's cold hand.

"I think it was a test," Anna said. "Jake gave it to me and he wanted to see what I did. I refused it, of course, because it was too big and too much money when we had only been seeing each other for a few months. But he forced me to take it. I think it pleased him that I thought it was beautiful and besides being concerned about how much money he was spending on me, I didn't focus on how much it was worth. To me, it was a symbol of his love and commitment. We got engaged shortly thereafter and he gave me a significantly sized engagement ring, but the cocktail ring was always my favorite."

I glanced at her engagement ring, which was still prominently displayed on the thin ring finger on her left hand. She was right; it was what I would consider ginormous. The large diamond was surrounded by rings and rings of diamonds and I'm sure when the light hit it, it would shine like the sun.

"It is preposterously large," Anna said with a smile when she noticed that I was looking at the ring. "But Jake said it was important to him to have it this large. He said that coming from a small town, keeping up appearances was important and was something he couldn't just stop doing. So I agreed to keep this ring, even though I would have preferred something much more streamlined."

I had to chuckle a little bit. No one ever really leaves a small town, not really. You could travel the world and still have those nagging thoughts in the back of your head, especially now with social media. Even when I was living the high life in the big city, one titch of gossip on social media would send me scouring for more and chatting about it with my sisters and Mandy. Small town appearances and gossip are sticky traps that are hard to leave, no matter how much distance you put between you and the town.

"I think that's a wonderful story," I said with a smile. Anna smiled back and I felt like it was the right time to tell her a little bit about myself. "You know, I lost my husband too. His name was Peter and he was killed in a car accident one morning on his way to work."

The memories came flooding back and this time I let them. I had been pushing them back too long and it felt good to let someone else hear about Peter. I w anted to connect with Anna to let her know she wasn't all alone.

"It's been a little over a year now, but it still seems fresh," I said. I let myself cry a little before I continued on. "I guess I just wanted to tell you that I get what you are going through and it is so hard and it doesn't go away, but it does get better. It gets easier. It won't seem like that now, but I can assure you it will. And if you ever need to talk to someone who understands, I would be happy to listen."

Anna's eyes shone and she leaned forward to wrap me in a hug. It seemed like an eternity that she and I sat intertwined in a hug, two young widows, one with fresh grief and one with grief that was only slightly scabbed over. We both cried until finally it felt like we had both let out all of the tears we needed to.

"Thank you, Tessa," Anna whispered. "Thank you for telling me about Peter. I appreciate everything you're doing right now for me."

I nodded and stood up, offering Anna my hand to help her stand up as well. The blanket we had been using to cover Jake's body was next to me. I picked it up and offered it to Anna, but she shook her head. I gently covered him up, tucking him in like a child.

Turning to Anna, I gave her a small smile. "Let's go find your ring," I said.

•Chapter Twenty-One•

Once again I found myself in the kitchen. This time I was debriefing Mandy on my conversation with Anna. I was also trying really hard not to pour myself another cup of coffee because if I did, I was pretty sure my bloodstream would be mostly caffeine at that point.

"How come you get to do all of the exciting stuff?" Mandy asked. "Nothing happened in the living room while you were gone. I mean, except for Chelsea trying so hard to sit on Clark's lap, but he kept pushing her away."

"Mandy, you hate doing this stuff," I said. "You hate true crime and I was back with a dead body. Do you really think you wanted to switch spots with me?"

"No," Mandy admitted after a moment. "I think I'm just getting bored."

This did not come as a surprise to me as Mandy was the sort of woman who was always bustling about, working on something or other. She flitted around working on project after project, making me feel like an utter failure. But here in the B&B, she was mostly stuck. No Donut Hut to look after. No Trevor to clean up behind. Just a dead body and a best friend who was playing private investigator.

The door between the living room and kitchen pushed open and Dawn came in, looking almost more irate as she had when I left to search for the ring in Jake's pocket. I still needed to search the dining room for the ring, but that would have to wait until I figured out what was going on with Dawn.

"May we help you?" I asked, putting on my syrupy customer service voice to try and mask my annoyance. It must not have worked because Mandy shot me a glance, but Dawn didn't seem to notice.

"Yes you may," Dawn said. "I think you need to be a little smarter during this entire investigation. You were just back there with his widow tampering with the body. How are we supposed to know that you didn't plant evidence or something?"

As Dawn raged on about incompetent investigating, she started to pace up and down the kitchen, waving her hands around. A glimmer from one of her hands caught my eye, but I couldn't quite focus on it because she was moving around too much.

"Calm down Dawn," I said. "Do you have

any ideas?"

The invitation for her to speculate about the case a little seemed to calm her down. Dawn slowed down her pacing and moved closer to Mandy and I.

"Yes, in fact, I do," Dawn said. "Now I think Lyle is a strong suspect, but I think you are overlooking someone else who I strongly suspect was involved. Someone who has quite the sob story to cover for her now."

I gasped involuntarily, aghast at the idea that she thought Anna would use grief to mask her guilt. But Dawn was totally serious about it. She stared into my eyes as she walked closer.

"I think that you are letting your own circumstances cloud your judgment," she said. Dawn kept moving towards me, sticking out her pointer finger until it was poking me in the chest. "You are letting your own grief take over and she is going to get away with murder because of it."

Anger was starting to fill me up. It felt like it was being sucked up through a straw, starting at my feet and moving slowly up. But before it could reach the top of my head, I looked down and realized that Dawn was wearing a blue emerald cocktail ring on the bony finger that was poking accusations into my chest.

I looked from the ring back up into her eyes and as recognition flooded her brown eyes, I grabbed her hand before she could put it down. Immediately she realized her mistake and tried to pull her hand away, but I kept a firm grip on her hand.

"Mandy, get Anna," I demanded. "Now!"

Without stopping to ask what in the world had gotten me so riled up, she zipped into the living room and came back with a very confused Anna.

"Anna, would this be the ring that we couldn't find on Jake's body?" I asked, shoving Dawn's hand towards her.

Anna's eyes widened in shock before they narrowed again with suspicion and anger. Dawn violently shook me off of her hand and pulled it back, not attempting to hide it, but certainly trying to get it out of sight. She started pacing again and agitation was flowing off of her.

"Why do you have my ring?" Anna asked, her voice quivering.

"Your ring?" Dawn said, her mouth twirling into an evil sneer. "Ha! This was my ring first. And I hated it. Jake had so much money and he gave me that stupid thing? I would have preferred a diamond."

"But it isn't yours anymore," Anna said. "Jake gave it to me and I loved it. Did you take it off of his dead body?"

Dawn huffed a few times as she tried to figure out how to spin this story to her advantage. No matter how you look at it, she had gone through a dead man's pockets and she took something that didn't belong to her, even if it had once upon a time.

"I need it more than you do even if it isn't worth that much.," Dawn said. "Besides, how do we know you weren't the one to kill him?"

"How dare you accuse me of killing Jake," Anna said. Tears were welling up in her eyes, but she was clenching her fists in anger. "Especially after you were blackmailing him. We found your note in his pocket. You were trying to get more money from him and you were doing it by faking your divorce to him? How dare you ruin our marriage just because you thought you deserved more money. If there is anyone here who should be watching their back, it is you."

I glanced at Mandy, who looked just as surprised as I was. I could understand the anger towards Dawn, but making threats against her probably wasn't the best recourse for Anna. Now I really wasn't sure what I thought.

"Don't you threaten me," Dawn said. "Here, you can have your stupid ring. It isn't worth that much anyways."

Dawn wrenched the cocktail ring off of her finger and threw it towards Anna, who easily caught it. I was a little bit impressed by her quick reflexes, but I tried not to let my face show it.

"I'll be up in my room if you need me," Dawn said.

She shoved her way through the door to the living room and stomped off. For a moment, none of us dared move or even breathe. The only sound was the wind outside, still gusting by. I finally broke the silence.

"Anna, are you okay?" I asked.

"I think so," she said. "I mean, I have the ring back. I'm not sure how I feel about everything else though."

"Can I ask you a tough question Anna?" I asked.

She nodded and I tried not to look at her sad face as I asked her my question. I knew it would hurt her and it was something that I don't think she had even thought about yet, but it was a realization that I had just had.

"If Dawn and Jake weren't technically divorced then that means that your marriage to Jake is not legal," I started out, trying to lead up to the question gently. "So now that Jake has died, wouldn't his money automatically go to Dawn?"

Anna looked dumbstruck. Her mouth was moving, but no sound was coming out. Mandy looked horrified that I had dared to ask that question. She kept blinking so much that it looked like her eyes were spasming. She was loudly chewing a piece of gum she had managed to find somewhere.

"I, I, I guess so," Anna finally stammered out. "I've lost everything then. My husband, our money, our things. What am I going to do?"

Mandy moved across the room and put her arm around Anna's shoulders. She gave her a squeeze while she sent a glare my way. Anna looked like she was frozen in time and I was the evil sorceress who had done the freezing. My heart sank down to my toes as Anna's entire world crumbled around her.

"I'm going to take Anna out to the living

room to give her some time to think,"
Mandy said.

I nodded as Mandy practically pushed
Anna back through the door to the living
room. That worked out fine for me because
I had other things I needed to do with all of
this new information.

•Chapter Twenty-Two•

After a quick check-in with Lyle and Claudia to make sure they were doing alright in the dining room, I brought my flashlight upstairs where I knocked on the door to Dawn's room. I waited for a moment before knocking again. This time, I could hear footsteps coming towards the door.

"Who is it?" Dawn's voice came muffled through the door.

"It's me, Tessa," I said. "I came to ask you a few questions."

I sensed some hesitation on the other side of the door, but after a moment, I heard the lock turn and the door cracked open. I gently pushed it and slid in. Dawn immediately slammed the door shut and locked it again.

"I feel like whoever killed Jake might come after me next," she said. "Mostly because I think Anna was the one who killed him and we both heard her threaten me."

I gently took Dawn's arm and walked her further into her room, guiding her to one of the two chairs. Her guest room was one of the smallest, but there was still a little seating area in a corner next to a window with two armchairs and a small table in between.

"Okay Dawn," I said once we were settled into the old but surprisingly comfortable armchairs. "Start at the beginning and tell me why you think Anna is the killer."

Dawn gave me a suspicious look, but launched into her reasoning. As she spoke, I could feel her sincerity. She seemed like she really believed everything she was saying.

"I have a few different reasons," she said. "Did you know that Anna has a boyfriend? I overheard Jake telling her that he was tired of her seeing someone else. He sounded pretty angry about it, so there's your motive. Plus, she didn't know that they weren't legally married, so she probably thought she could get away with it and get everything. She probably thought she'd have all of the money and her boyfriend too. Pretty sweet deal, especially when you don't have to deal with that jerk anymore."

Anna had told me that Jake knew about the boyfriend and was okay with it, but Dawn says she heard that he wasn't. At this point, it was she said, she said. I wasn't sure who to believe, but it did poke a hole in

181

Anna's story.

"The other thing is that she could have saved him," Dawn said. "What took her so long to get his medicine? He always kept it in that pouch and I have a hard time thinking that he didn't show her where it was when he got here. When we were together, he was always very careful to have his injectors somewhere nearby and he always showed me where they were."

"So you think that Anna may have just been lying when she said she couldn't find them?" I asked. I hated to doubt Anna, but Dawn made a good point.

"I don't just think so, I'm pretty sure she is," Dawn said. "And I know she seems extra sad, but remember, she does work in showbiz. Anna may be mostly a dancer, but she is also an actress."

I mulled all of this over in my mind, being more confused than ever about all of this. I could think of one more person I should talk to, but I really didn't want to. Clark had accompanied Anna up to the honeymoon suite to help her find the medicine. He would be the best person to ask about what she had been doing up there. I thought briefly about having Mandy question him but as the unofficial lead investigator in this murder, I suppose I'd have to suck it up and be the one to ask him.

"Anything else you want to say before I go?" I asked.

"Yes, one more," she said. "I know you think I'm a scumbag for all of this. I know it seems terrible, but I'm still reeling from all of this. I loved Jake once, but I got tired of living with a jerk. He was critical of my appearance and the fact that he thought I didn't try hard enough to look 'Hollywood' for him. He scrutinized anything I spent money on. And he could be downright cruel. I felt trapped and I ended up gaining weight and all Jake could do was mock me."

Dawn's mousy face scrunched up as she started to cry. I reached over and handed her a tissue from the box next to me.

"In the end, he decided I wasn't good enough to be his wife," she said as she wiped her cheeks. "So he divorced me. But I got the last laugh because I never signed the papers. So his marriage to that bimbo is a total sham."

Dawn laughed a shaky laugh that disgusted me. Obviously I don't condone Jake's behavior towards her, but to ruin his life like this was totally uncalled for. I felt like no one involved in this entire business was very likable.

I left Dawn's room, hearing the bolt slide shut as I walked down the hallway. But instead of going downstairs with everyone else, I headed to my room. I needed a little time to think.

My room was cold and even though I never made my bed, Mandy always made hers. And since my bed had been her bed last night, that meant my bed was nicely made. I smiled as I plopped down on top of it and wrapped myself in a nice fuzzy blanket that Mandy had neatly folded and placed on the foot of the bed.

Solving this murder was completely draining the energy out of me. It wasn't even the lack of sleep and electricity either. It was the sheer fact that the world was full of gray. There were no good or bad people in this scenario that was playing out. Instead, there were people that were shades of gray. They all had some sort of sob story that was wrapped up in their own nasty behavior. Add that to the fact that Jake hadn't exactly been a nice person himself and I've got a mystery that I didn't really feel like solving.

In fact at this point, I felt like the only

reason I was all wrapped up in this was because I had to be. I was stuck here and someone had to figure out what had happened to Jake because the police couldn't get here to do it themselves. I would have washed my hands of it long ago if I could have.

I set my flashlight on my nightstand, standing up so that the beam made a bright circle on the ceiling. Since I was here, I really just needed a few minutes to lay here by myself and think. As I lay back, the fatigue I had been ignoring all day washed over me and I decided that it would be okay to close my eyes, just for a little while.

•Chapter Twenty-Three•

My eyes flew open. It was pitch black in my room. I looked over at my flashlight which I had purposely left on, but it was dark. I grabbed it and the metal was cool in my hand. I pushed the button, but nothing happened. I clicked it a few more times, but the batteries must have died while I was sleeping.

My heart started pounding so hard it was almost coming out of my chest. I was sure I looked like one of those cartoon characters except my heart wasn't pounding because I was so in love. My heart was pounding because absolute terror was taking hold of me.

I was alone and I was in the dark. The room felt like it was closing in on me. I tried to look out the window to help ground myself, but there was no light out there. Everything was obscured by the storm that was still raging. I felt like I was trapped in this room and that I would be trapped forever, never able to leave this dark, cramped space. Normally my room felt small and cozy, but when it was plunged into the darkness, it felt all-consuming and full of danger.

Sweat was covering my body and I started to feel frantic. The dark was starting to consume me and I tried to take a deep breath so that I could think. I usually kept extra batteries and an extra flashlight under my bed. I needed to find it before I passed out from lack of oxygen.

I rolled off my bed, collapsing onto the floor as I was gasping for breath. There was a small tote under my bed where I kept my extras and I reached into the dark abyss of under the bed and pulled it out. I ripped the top off of the bin, trying my hardest to slow down my breathing and stay somewhat calm.

There was no extra flashlight in my bin and I remembered that I had added it to the assortment of flashlights we had handed out to everyone. That was okay, I just needed to replace the batteries in the flashlight I already had. There were four batteries in the bin, but I only needed two.

I grabbed the top of the flashlight and screwed off the top, dumping the batteries onto my carpet. With sweaty, shaky hands, I grabbed two batteries and shoved them into the flashlight chamber. It took me a few times to line the top back on and screw it back on, but as soon as it tightened up, I started to feel a twinge of relief at the possibility of filling this dark space of light soon.

I pushed the rubber button in, but nothing happened. The room stayed pitch black and any bit of relief rushed out of me once again. I shook the flashlight, pushing the button frantically in and out. These batteries must be dead also. I tried to calm myself, no need to panic.

There were still two more batteries in the bin, so I took as big of a breath as I was able and set about replacing the batteries once again. My hands were so sweaty and shaky that I had to use my sweatshirt to help me get a grip so that I could twist open the flashlight. I spilled the old batteries out and once again shoved the two last batteries in. I tried to focus all of my attention on my task and ignore the fact that somehow the darkness seemed to somehow be getting darker and thicker.

Once again, nothing happened when I pressed the button. I wanted to cry, but the fear overtaking me stopped the tears from falling. Any sadness was pushed back by the fear. It was consuming everything in me, even my other emotions.

I was an idiot, plain and simple. These were old batteries and for some reason I had shoved them back in the bin instead of throwing them away. It was something I hadn't even considered that someday I would be in an emergency like this and those old batteries would be what pushed me over the edge into a heaving, shaking panic attack.

The shaking that had started in my hands was traveling throughout my own body now. I couldn't stop trembling as the dark pushed in on me even more. I knew that I just had to find my way out of here and back down to the living room, but that seemed absolutely impossible right now. I brought my knees up and wrapped my arms around them, putting my forehead down.

As I shakily tried to take deep breaths, a small sound caught my attention in the hall. I wasn't sure if I was hearing things simply because of the dark that was pressing in or if there was someone out there. I tried as hard as I could to breathe as quietly as possible.

There was the sound again. Someone was coming down the hallway, I just knew it. I could tell that whoever was out there was trying their hardest to be quiet. But who was it? Why were they sneaking around?

Suddenly, the doorknob on my room was rattled as whoever was on the other side was trying to open the door. I focused on it, sure that I was hallucinating this. I was focusing so hard that it actually was helping me calm down just enough to pull me back from the brink of a panic attack.

But then the doorknob was rattled again. Someone was trying to get in here and I don't think the tiny lock on the doorknob would be enough to stop whoever was out there. Even though they were being as stealthy as possible, there was a determination out there that was seeping through the locked door.

I opened my mouth and the most bloodcurdling scream I've ever heard erupted from deep inside of me. It almost seemed like it was coming from someone else. But I couldn't stop. It rolled out of me like the shrieking wind outside and a small piece of me hoped someone would hear it and know it was me and not the blizzard that was still raging outside.

•Chapter Twenty-Four•

It seemed like I sat there for hours, my voice growing hoarse as I screamed. But soon enough, I could hear people coming down the hallway again. This time, they were thundering instead of sneaking and I had to assume it wasn't whoever had been coming for me before.

"Tessa, are you in there?" came Mandy's voice as fists started to pound on my door. "Open up. The door is locked so we can't open it."

I took as deep a breath as I could and walked over to the door, turning the doorknob just enough to unlock it. I stepped back and the door burst open revealing everyone who was staying at the bed and breakfast, all of them holding bright flashlights that filled my room with light.

Suddenly, everything felt better. My room was back to feeling cozy rather than full of an overwhelming darkness that was pushing in on me. My father was suddenly standing in front of me with his arms out and I collapsed into them. Now the tears started to flow.

191

For a while, everyone allowed me to work through the tears, murmuring to each other as they wondered what was happening. Then Mandy appeared at my father's side, putting her hand gently on my arm.

"Tessa, what happened?" she asked gently.

I took a deep breath and told them everything that had happened, from my falling asleep and waking up to the flashlight batteries being dead to whoever had tried to open my door.

"Do you think it was the killer trying to get you?" Dawn asked, her dark eyes opening wide.

"Don't be silly, I'm sure she was imagining it," Chelsea said. Clark gave her a slightly horrified look but for once I don't think she was trying to be mean. She looked genuinely scared, her red hair flying everywhere. By writing off my fears, she was trying to make herself feel better. And I really couldn't blame her.

"Why don't we all move back downstairs and try to calm down a bit," my mother said from the back of the group. "We can get some coffee and snacks out for anyone who would like them."

Almost as one, the group turned around and started back down the hallway, taking most of the light with them. Clark hesitated for a moment, but Chelsea grabbed his arm and pulled him along. He shot a guilty glance at me, but allowed himself to be pulled away.

I was left in my room with my father and Mandy, one on either side of me. For a moment, we all stood in silence as I continued to slow down my breathing. I was almost back to what I would consider my normal state.

"Are you alright?" my father asked once again. There was concern in his eyes that was apparent even in the low light. No matter how old I got, I was always his baby.

"I'm fine," I said. "Can I ask you all to do one thing? Can you leave me a flashlight and go downstairs without me."

"Are you sure?" Mandy asked. "That doesn't seem right."

"I need to make sure I can be comfortable in my own room again," I said. "And I need to do that by myself."

My father and Mandy glanced at each other and after a moment, Mandy handed over the flashlight she was holding. After another moment of hesitation, they both walked out my bedroom door and into the hallway, glancing back over their shoulders to make sure I was okay.

"I'll be okay now that I have the flashlight," I said.

I nodded at them both with a small smile on my face, hoping they would see that the fear had been pushed back down. As they left, I sat back down on my bed, taking a deep breath. I slowly moved the flashlight around the room, letting myself get reacquainted with all of the corners of my cozy room.

Once I had looked around the entire space with the flashlight all while taking deep breaths, I was back to feeling like my calm self. I was ready to rejoin the world of downstairs but as I stood up, I wondered if I was ready to keep investigating. What if the killer had been the one coming down the hallway?

For now, I just needed to rejoin the little world of the bed and breakfast. I gripped the flashlight tightly as I left my room and started down the hallway but before I could get far, a glint caught my eye.

The beam of light from the flashlight was hitting something on the floor and reflecting back. I hadn't noticed it before, so I had to assume that it hadn't been there for long. All of a sudden, I felt suspicious. I glanced around to make sure no one else was there, but I was all alone. I crept towards the glint and knelt down.

There on the rug that ran down the middle of the hallway was a gold ring. I reached out to pick it up but just as I was about to touch it, I pulled back. What was I doing? This may be potential evidence. I couldn't just pick it up and contaminate it. I dashed into my room and grabbed a tissue.

This time, I picked it up with the tissue, careful not to touch it with my skin. It was a thick gold ring that appeared to be a men's wedding band. I turned it around a few times, but it was just plain gold. Then I noticed that the inside appeared to have an inscription.

I grasped the ring through the tissue in one hand and got the flashlight as close to it as I could so that I could read it. The inscription was really small and I was holding the ring so close to my face to try and read it that I actually held my breath, concerned that somehow breathing on the ring could transfer tiny bits of my DNA on it. I squinted until I could read the small, scrawling inscription.

To my Jakers from your Anna Banana

How in the world had Jake's wedding ring made it all the way up to our personal, family area of the B&B? He had certainly never been up here while he was alive or dead. I sat back on my heels and thought for a moment. Did this mean that whoever was up here trying to get into my room was the killer?

The realization was washing over me that whoever killed Jake may have been trying to kill me just now. Usually in the crime movies that I watched that meant the detective was getting too close to figuring the case out. But I absolutely was not close to figuring it out. I had no idea who did it and every time I thought I was close, something else came up that totally contradicted it.

I stood up and walked back to my room. I wrapped the ring up in a tissue and hid it underneath the socks in the middle drawer of my dresser. It would need to be dealt with later, but for now I just could not deal with another clue that just added more confusion to the case. I especially could not deal with it up here, by myself, in the dark.

Slamming the dresser drawer shut, I scurried back down the hallway and towards the sanctuary of downstairs. I wasn't sure what to think about being back with everyone else. It meant that I was safe and unsafe all at once as I still didn't know who did it. I just hoped the police would be here soon to help me.

•Chapter Twenty-Five•

The living room was quietly bustling once again, but it all felt so suspicious to me now. I almost felt like I couldn't rule anyone out. What if there as something I was missing? What if someone I had ruled out had some sort of secret connection to Jake and a motive to kill him? I felt totally lost and I wondered if I was just incompetent. I've solved things before, so I've never doubted my powers of deduction. But now I just can't quite keep it all together.

The chair in the library corner where I sat was secluded and felt just right for this moment in time where I needed to pull myself together. This time, Mandy took one look at me and knew that I wanted space, so she gave me a small smile and sat on the floor in front of the fireplace instead.

Anna was sitting near Mandy on the floor, warming herself up. I watched her and wondered if maybe she was the killer. Who else would have taken Jake's wedding ring off of his body, especially one inscribed with such a personal message.

Dawn's voice started ringing through my head. She had accused me of being blind to the fact that Anna was the killer because I was also a young widow. Was she right? Was I looking past obvious facts because I identified with the position that Anna was now in? I ran through the clues in my head. The wedding ring would be an obvious thing for Anna to take. She also had taken too long to find Jake's medication. But the fish sauce bottle had still been found in Lyle's room.

Anna was sitting on the floor and even though she was surrounded by people, she wasn't interacting with anyone. My heart went out to her because I really did identify with her. The widow club is a club that no one ever wants to join but once you are in, you feel so deeply for anyone else in the club. And I had a hard time imagining that Anna not only killed Jake, but could also act so distraught over his loss that it would pull the wool over my eyes.

Everyone else was acting fairly normal, although they were a bit leery of the fact that I had asked Lyle, Claudia, and Tank to join us back in the living room. There was just enough of a cloud of suspicion over other people that I couldn't justify making him stay separate from us. Plus, we had Tank here. If Lyle tried anything, Tank would be able to subdue him.

As I watched the two older couples finish another puzzle at the table and various people slowly leaf through their books as they read, I made a decision to just quit investigating. That was it. I was just going to be done looking into it. All it was doing was dredging up hurtful memories of Peter and making me lose sleep. Besides, the police would be here soon enough and they could take it off of my hands.

Until then, I decided, I would read a book. I needed something to take my mind off of this situation. I reached back and grabbed a book without looking at the title. A surprise of a different variety would be nice.

Instead, I was greeted with a detective novel, which was just the universe's way of mocking me. I groaned quietly and dropped the book on the floor. I ventured to the coffee table avoiding everyone's glances, and blindly grabbed a handful of magazines from on top.

Plopping back into my armchair, I realized I had grabbed a thrilling array of titles including *Birds Monthly*, *Minnesota Wildlife,* and *Leisurely Golf Lifestyle.* I closed my eyes and selected one at random.

As I leafed through and learned more about Minnesota nature and animals than I ever thought I would know, I felt myself dozing off again. I wasn't the only one. My father was asleep in his arm chair and both Dave and Joe looked like if they were anywhere more comfortable than the folding chairs they were currently sitting on to dismantle the puzzle, they would be asleep also.

I glanced at the clock on the mantle, which was an old clock that had to be wound and therefore was the only clock still working in the living room. It said that it was only mid-afternoon. It was that time of day where it was too early to eat dinner, but also a bit too late to have a snack just in case the snack would be too big and spoil your dinner. Unfortunately that meant there wasn't any cooking I could do to distract myself.

I usually prided myself as being someone with a rich inner life who was never actually bored. But swearing off investigating this murder must have meant that the me that existed in my rich inner life was upset. My mind kept drifting back to the clues that didn't fit together. No matter how I tried to think about other things or play games with myself, it was just those darn clues that kept floating back in.

There were actually a few articles in the magazines I had chosen that were somewhat interesting. They held my attention enough that I was able ignore the fact that Chelsea was in some sort of slow chase with Clark around the living room.

Every time Clark would choose a place to sit down, Chelsea would appear next to him and try to practically sit on top of him. Clark would shift or move casually to another spot and soon enough, Chelsea would appear soon after. It was a bit comical for me to watch.

At first, it only happened every few minutes, but I could see Clark getting more and more upset about it. I watched over the top of my magazine as he finally got so sick of it that he started walking laps around the living room and when that didn't stop her from following him, he came up with an even better plan.

As I watched, he noticed that Anna and Mandy were sitting on the floor in front of the fireplace with just a small space between them. On his next lap around the living room, he suddenly plopped down and wedged himself in between the two women.

Poor Anna didn't even seem to notice what was happening, but Mandy had also been watching this entire escapade and once Clark was next to her, Mandy actually moved even closer to him so that Chelsea would have nowhere to go.

Chelsea stopped in her tracks, contemplating her next move. I looked around the living room to see that by now, everyone was surreptitiously watching her. Dawn was doing the worst job of it, barely covering her snickering sneer with her hand as she openly watched the spectacle.

Once Chelsea realized that no matter what she did, there was no way she was going to be able to squeeze in, she stomped back to the couch where she sat with her arms crossed and the biggest stink face I've ever seen an adult wear.

At first, I felt bad about Anna getting roped into this ridiculous game of cat and mouse, but when I looked at her I could see just the faintest glimmer of a grin on her face and realized that even though she was pretending not to notice what was going on, she was a willing participant.

It felt good to see her smile, even though I was having some doubts about her grief. I felt terrible questioning whether or not her grief was genuine. I felt like I would rather believe she was grieving and be wrong rather than assume it was fake and find out she wasn't the killer and her grief was real.

All I could think about was how hurtful it would be if someone had questioned my grief. Of course, Peter was killed in a car accident whereas Jake was murdered and we still didn't know who did it. Those situations were so vastly different that I couldn't really compare myself to Anna.

I noticed that I kept circling around to myself. Maybe Dawn was right. Maybe I was making this all about myself without even realizing it.

•Chapter Twenty-Six•

I finished all of the magazines I could find on the coffee table, really wishing that those trashy magazines I had seen upstairs would have been here instead. As much as I love reading about birds, I would have enjoyed reading celebrity gossip just a bit more.

The clock over the fireplace was slowly, slowly marching towards dinnertime but it was still too early to think about the food. Time felt like it was going so slowly that I might be stuck in a time loop. The only indication that I wasn't stuck in a time loop was the fact that the clock had been slowly moving.

I was bored of sitting so I stood up and strolled towards the picture window. So far the storm had been raging so hard that we couldn't even see the bird feeders that sat just a few yards outside of the living room. But when I walked up to the window, I could just barely make them out.

"Hey, I think the snow might be dying down," I called out to no one in particular.

Everyone rushed to the window like a bunch of school kids watching the first snowflakes of winter. We all squeezed together to try and determine if the storm was stopping or if maybe the winds were just shifting a bit.

"I don't think it's dying down at all," said with a sneer. "It is still blowing just as much as it was before.

"No it isn't," Mandy said. "You can actually see the bird feeders now. Before you couldn't see them at all."

"But look at how much the wind is blowing the tree branches," Cheryl said. "It is still super windy out there."

"Do you think the police will actually be able to make it here now?" Anna whispered.

"I think they are trying their hardest," I said.

As the discussion about whether the storm was dying down continued, I walked back a few steps and took a look at the group I'd been stuck with during this storm. Here everyone was standing together in front of the picture window and I marveled at how people who were forced to spend so much time together could still stand to be so close together. I tried to look at the group with fresh eyes.

The two older couples were still laughing together about the grand adventure they had ended up on, stuck in the B&B during a blizzard. Lyle had joined the group at the window, but before he had been loud and full of anger. Now he was quiet and just trying to be part of the group. Claudia was holding Lyle's hand, quietly showing that she was standing with him even though he had been accused of murder.

Dawn was standing off to the side, close enough to Anna to make me wonder if that felt awkward for them, but far enough away that Anna didn't seem to notice Dawn. Tank was standing behind Anna. Now that he wasn't protecting the top suspect, it almost seemed like he had made it his unofficial job to keep an eye on Anna. The thought sprung to mind that he was either protecting a grieving widow or a guilty suspect, but I pushed that back down.

kept trying to grab Clark's hand and even after he crossed his arms to hide his hands, she grabbed his elbow. She had shown me up by kissing him in my house and she was determined not to let him go. It was almost as if she was scared that if she let him go, he would come running back to me.

I kind of wanted to tell her that it wasn't going to happen. I can't say that I wouldn't ever go out with him again, but I can say that it would certainly take some convincing for me to want to give him another chance. As I looked at Clark, I still thought he was gorgeously handsome, but other than that, I didn't feel that twinge that I used to. I guess that's what happens when you find your guy kissing someone else in your kitchen.

I tried not to think about everything that Clark had said to me. All of this time I had been dating him, I had been filled with anxiety and nerves about whether I was worthy enough to date such a handsome man. But he had seen right through me without me even realizing it.

What hit me the hardest was that he was totally right about everything. I could understand why he was annoyed. He felt like he needed to be constantly reassuring me and I could see why that was so annoying. In that moment, I felt bad. Here I had been upset when really we both had a right to be upset.

"I'm going to turn on the weather radio again," my dad said.

He ventured into the kitchen and returned with a little brown box with a knob on top. Thankfully it had batteries, so once he set it down and turned the knob, a mechanical computer voice came out of the little speaker.

Winter Storm Paul is still moving southwest over Shady Lake. Expect a small break in the storm before one more round comes down.

A collective groan filled the room as the computer voice moved into the seven day forecast. I didn't care about the fact that it was supposed to be warm and sunny a few days from now. I cared more that the storm wasn't actually over.

"Sorry everyone," I said with a shrug. "I thought it might be winding down. Apparently I was wrong."

"You didn't know," my mother said. "We were all hoping that it was almost over."

Slowly, everyone drifted back to their respective places in the living room. I wondered how many jigsaw puzzles the group in the corner had finished during this blizzard. I almost didn't want to know because it already felt like we had been stuck here for days.

I took my time to look around the group one more time and I finalized my decision. I was going to stop investigating. And I wasn't just going to say that but keep thinking about the murder. It was going to be shoved out of my mind and if I found myself thinking about it, I would stop it immediately.

Here was a wonderful blizzard that was making such a cozy situation and instead of being contented in my introverted heart, I was driving myself crazy trying to solve what was turning into an unsolvable murder. And I was done with it. I was done investigating and thinking about clues and suspects.

My mind felt so free suddenly. I hadn't even realized how much space all of the pieces of the murder were taking up. I sat back in my chair and exhaled, a feeling of calm washing over me.

Maybe this was what it was like to be someone else like Mandy who didn't care about true crime although, I suppose, the space in my mind that I usually dedicate to crime was probably dedicated to something like donuts in Mandy's mind. I needed something to fill that spot in my mind and it couldn't be donuts.

•Chapter Twenty-Seven•

For a while, I sat and did absolutely nothing. It felt amazing and I realized that I needed to do this more often. My mind was so cluttered usually and from what I heard all of the time on the news, the modern age attributed to that. I had given up one thing that everyone loved to malign, which was the smartphone.

I used to be attached to my smartphone, but when Peter died, I didn't want to lose myself in technology. I was finding myself going down the internet rabbit hole whenever I started to feel sad. There had been a realization that if I kept doing that, I'd never be able to actually deal with my grief. I would be stuck forever because I never actually dealt with it.

Instead, I got rid of my smartphone and downgraded to a flip phone, which I considered a dumb phone. It also meant that I hardly ever used social media anymore. Now that I couldn't access it any time I pulled my phone out of my pocket, I kind of forgot to check it.

Mandy was the one that was addicted to her smartphone and social media. I tried to tell her that once, but she didn't want to hear it. Mandy didn't like to admit it, but she was a bit of a gossip. She said she only shared things that she knew for sure were truth but even if she only passed on truth, she was still gossiping.

I didn't really understand why you needed social media once you lived in a small town. All you had to do was go out and about and you heard all of the gossip. You didn't need to take your phone out and scroll through social media because you could hear it all when you were picking out your groceries or shopping for a new blouse.

"Stop putting those together," Joe was saying. "We need to finish the outside edges first."

"Does it really matter if the puzzle gets put together?" Cheryl said.

The puzzle group seemed to be starting to fall out. Counting the boxes on the floor, it seemed like they had put together something like four big puzzles since we realized we were stuck in the blizzard. I was actually a little surprised that it took that many puzzles for them to start bickering.

", I need some space," Clark said. He was

trying to talk quietly, but we were all shoved together in this one room so his voice carried.

I tried not to smile as I had been wondering at what point would Clark's politeness wear off. had been relentless in her pursuit of Clark. I know that when I wasn't around just acted like a normal date, but since she had been stuck with me around for the past almost two days, she had turned into some kind of crazed 'gimme-gimme' girl.

Clark had been putting up with it well enough, but he was finally not only getting tired of it, he was getting tired of being polite about it.

"Oh come on, Clarky," she cooed. I had to cringe. sounded like some sort of character from a bad movie from the 1950's. "I just want to sit next to you."

"If that was true, that would be fine," he said. "But you want to sit on top of me. No thanks. I know it is a bit chilly in here, but then get a blanket."

pouted and slunk away, grabbing a blanket out of the basket. Making a big show of wrapping it around herself, she perched on the end of the sofa. When she noticed me watching her, she scowled at me. I stuck my tongue out at her before I could stop myself. was so surprised that she forgot to keep the scowl on her face. I tried not to laugh at her anymore. I know it was juvenile, but it felt really good.

"Please stop staring at us," Claudia said, interrupting the relative quiet.

We all looked around at each other, trying to figure out who she was talking to. No one was looking particularly guilty, so I couldn't tell.

"Who are you talking to?" Tank finally said.

"I'm talking to Dawn," she said. "I know you guys suspect that Lyle was the one who killed Jake, but he didn't do it. You can stop staring at us like we are going to suddenly whip out a gun and start shooting. Besides, as far as I can tell, there are serious doubts about Lyle being the killer. If they still thought he was the one, we would still be sitting by ourselves in the dining room."

"I haven't been staring at you," Dawn said, her eyes going wide. Something about her expression seemed to be put on, like she was acting surprised for show. "I've just been trying to figure out who did it, just like everyone else here."

"Well you can stop staring at us," Claudia

said. "I'm tired of it."

Before Dawn could speak up again, my father rose to his feet. He commanded the attention of the room as he got up and walked to a spot in front of the fireplace.

"I think we all need to take it down a notch," he said. "We are all here together until this storm ends, so we may as well make the most of it. We need to prioritize staying warm and not driving each other nuts. If we actually knew who did it, that person wouldn't be here in this room. At this point, it will be up to the police when they are able to make it here."

The room quietly muttered along in agreement. My father slowly walked back, sat down in his chair and picked up the magazine about birds that he had been reading.

Everyone seemed to be getting more and more suspicious. It made me wonder if they just were curious to solve the crime or if they thought the killer may kill someone else and they wanted to be prepared. But, I had put that in the back of my mind.

Honestly, I was done and over it. Whoever had killed Jake wasn't someone who was going to kill anyone else. There was no reason to kill anyone else. So far, they had gotten away with it and somehow left clues that pointed to multiple different people. I had to tip my hat to whoever it was because they had either purposely planted clues or they had extraordinary luck during this entire fiasco.

Either way, no one else was in danger and my curiosity had reached the end. Until then, I would have to occupy myself with people-watching and magazine reading. I guess being stuck here in a blizzard wasn't so bad, unless you happened to be Jake.

•Chapter Twenty-Eight•

I continued my mostly surreptitious people watching for a little while as the tension in the room slowly mounted. This time, it wasn't because there was a killer in our midst. Rather, everyone was just starting to get sick of everyone else.

Here we all were, a bunch of relative strangers stuck in a bed and breakfast together during a blizzard and not only were we stuck in the same room simply for heating purposes, but someone here had already killed a guest. It was a recipe for disaster.

As time wore on, the bickering got worse and worse and the snide comments got louder and louder. Finally I felt like I was at a middle school hang out instead of stuck in a B&B during Valentine's Day weekend. If this blizzard lasted much longer, the police may find a mass murder after we all get sick of each other and bludgeon each other to death. I shook my head because I didn't think my black humor was appropriate in light of the situation with poor Jake. But being stuck like this made me turn to some morbid humor.

Thinking of the police made me think of Max and it was like he knew that because just then, Mandy walked over with her phone.

"I just got another message from Max for you," she said, handing me her phone.

Hey Mandy, just a message for Tessa. Tessa, can you let me know how things are going please? I haven't heard from you in a while.

I took the phone and started to type a message before I was interrupted by my mother.

"Okay everyone, I've had quite enough of all of the bickering," my mother said, clapping her hands together. "I haven't heard this many arguments since I had six children living here. So I have decided that we are putting together a board game tournament."

The inevitable groans and protests were quickly cut off by a wave of my mother's hand.

"None of that," she said. "I don't want to hear any complaining. I've given you all long enough to figure out a way to occupy your time and for a while it was okay. But now I'm sick of hearing all of the squabbles. So we are going to set up some tables and pick out a few board games and we are

218

going to round robin a competition and come up with an ultimate winner."

My mother stood in the doorway to the entryway as she announced her idea, looking both formidable enough that no one would refute her idea and also like a sweet old lady who just had a great idea. I had to admit that it was a good idea because we were all stuck together anyways. We may as well make the most of it.

My childhood had been filled with these sorts of ideas. My mother was great at coming up with creative ways to occupy our time if we didn't have our own ideas. The board game competition idea was a well tested idea that was used throughout our childhood whenever the weather was too terrible to go out. I was actually sort of excited that my mother had thought it could apply to this situation also.

"Great idea," I said, standing up. I wanted to make sure to throw support behind her right away so that the idea would gain more traction. "I think we are all thrilled to finally have an idea that will keep us busy through what is hopefully the last bit of this blizzard."

"I think that sounds great," Dave said from the table in the corner. "I think my eyesight is starting to go bad after squinting at all of these tiny puzzle pieces in the last two days. I'd much rather play board games."

He ceremoniously grabbed a large chunk of the partially-done puzzle and started breaking it back up into small piece in the box. I expected the rest of the puzzle crew to protest, but instead they laughed along and started to break up the rest of along with Dave.

Already, the idea of something new and fun was really helping to dissipate the tension in the room. Smiles were appearing on everyone's faces as they put down their books and magazines and started to talk with excitement.

I typed out a quick message for Max with a question that had been nagging at the back of my mind before handing the phone back to Mandy.

Everything is fine. We are back to square one, not knowing who killed Jake. I've decided not to keep investigating. We are having a board game competition instead. There is something I've been wondering about though. Dawn said she didn't sign the divorce papers, so she and Jake were still legally married and she will get everything in his estate. Is that really how it works?

Max sent back a quick reply that answered my question.

No, that is definitely not how it works. It only takes one signature.

That was kind of what I had thought, so I sent a quick message back.

I thought so. She is not going to be happy about that.

As I wondered who was going to break the news to Dawn that her debts would not be taken care of, Anna spoke up.

"What do we need to do to set everything up?" Anna said quietly.

She looked hopeful and I knew that she was hoping this competition could take her mind off of things. For her sake, I hoped that it would too.

But there I was, identifying with her once again. I just couldn't help but put myself into her shoes because I knew what it was like to be a young widow. I needed to stop because for all I know, she was the one who made herself a widow. My mind whirled around and around that idea.

I closed my eyes for a moment and reminded myself that I needed to stop thinking about the murder and anything having to do with it, especially Anna and her newly acquired widow status. Every time I thought about it, I could feel that idea dragging me closer and closer to the deep dark hole of grief. I managed to pull myself out of it this far but if I allowed myself to be continually dragged into grief, it would be harder and harder to get out each time.

Once, I heard an analogy for grief that I really enjoyed. It basically said that when a death first happens, carrying around the grief is like carrying around a huge camping style backpack of grief. But as time marches on, the luggage gets smaller and smaller until you are still carrying it around, but it is now the size of a small pocketbook with a shoulder strap. It is still always there with you, but much more manageable and small enough that you are able to forget you have it with you.

But since I've been trapped in this house with a new widow, every time I think of her or her grief, my grief has gotten larger and larger. I've been up-sizing my grief luggage each time and right now, it is noticeably larger than my usual pocketbook of grief. I needed to stop before I was dragging around a trunk of grief, allowing myself to live in the dark place instead of honoring Peter by going on to live my life as a still vibrant young woman.

After taking a few more deep breaths, I opened my eyes to find the living room bustling with activity. Mandy was watching me with some interest, her eyes narrowed as she tried to figure out what I was doing. I could see the concern playing in her eyes as she determined if she should come over to me or not. I shook my head just a tiny bit and gave her a small smile to let her know that I was okay. She smiled back and continued folding up blankets and putting them away.

I was going to throw myself whole-heartedly into this board game competition. I was going to push my grief back and focus on winning the whole darn thing.

•Chapter Twenty-Nine•

When we did board game competitions in our childhood, it was mostly a loosely set up way to make us spend a few hours without beating up on each other. We still managed to squabble and occasionally someone got angry enough to flip the board over, but mostly we kept busy and out of our mother's hair.

Now though, we had to come up with a better system because some of the more competitive adults were demanding a fair competition. So my mother and I put our heads together and came up with an entire afternoon's worth of gaming for everyone to enjoy.

We had four different board games that four different people at a time would play, rotating so that everyone played each game once plus one round of a break. The winner each time would receive five points, second place would get three points and third place would get one point with the loser receiving a big fat zero. At the very end, whoever had the most points would win the entire competition.

The setup was such that the same people

would not play each game with the same people. Everyone would rotate around and play with different people each game. We also chose an assortment of games that involved both skill and luck, so that it really was anyone's game.

The games were Chinese Checkers, Crazy Eights, Snakes and Ladders, and a trivia game. Everyone would play each game once. There was a mix of skill and luck and all of the games were pretty quick, so it wasn't like we were playing chess with a grand master or making everyone play a certain real estate buying board game for hours on end.

I scrounged up a piece of poster board from the area by the front desk that was supposed to be used for something else a few weeks from now, but we would have to buy another one because I made a giant grid on this one with everyone's names and the games where we could record how many points each person got each time.

The next thing we had to do was set up four different tables with the games. As a bed and breakfast, we had plenty of folding tables and chairs for the various events we hosted here. The only problem was that they were down in the basement, so I'd have to conquer my fears and head down there to get them.

I had one of my beloved flashlights and I roped Dawn and Mandy into going downstairs with me to collect everything. As we set off to haul up three more tables and countless more chairs, Clark hurried after us.

"Please let me help you, ladies," he said. He scurried around us and was the first to rush down the dark steps.

I turned around and saw a confused looking around, obviously looking for Clark. I laughed and hurried through the kitchen door, making sure didn't see Clark's back disappearing down the basement stairs.

The normally dark basement was now like a dark crypt without the light from the single hanging light bulb that we normally could switch on down there. I shivered as I showed everyone where the old folding tables and chairs were leaning up against one dank wall. At least when the light bulb was on, I could see into the corners of the basement. But with only flashlights to light the way, most of the concrete basement was swathed in darkness that couldn't be parted by the powerful beams.

Together, we hoisted the plastic and metal seating up the stairs and into the living room. Between the four of us, we were able to carry enough to only take one trip. I was grateful Clark had come along with us so that we didn't have to go back down into the darkness anymore.

The house was getting colder and colder the longer that the power was out, so we wanted to keep everyone in the living room so that the fire could warm everyone. We shoved the couch back against one of the bookcases and set up the three folding tables around the living room. Each table had four chairs around it. Along with the table that always sat in the corner by the windows, there would be enough space for everyone to play their games. Anyone who was on the one round where they weren't playing could sit on the couch and watch everyone else.

While we had been gathering up tables and chairs, my mother had been busy in the kitchen throwing together anything she could find for a strange dinner. At this point, it felt like we had eaten the same thing for all of our lunches and dinner since the blizzard started, but it was all that we had.

Trays of lunch meat and sliced cheese sat next to basket of bread and crackers. A bowl of guacamole was alongside a bag of tortilla chips and there was still a half-eaten vegetable tray with dip. There was also a tray of cookies along with carafes of hot water for tea or hot chocolate.

It wasn't much, but it would make a good dinner for everyone and hopefully by the time we got to lunch tomorrow at the latest, the storm will have died down enough for us to have the power back on so we could stop eating all of the food that the fridge had to offer.

The stove worked, since it was a gas stove, but we had eaten a lot of the other "simple" foods towards the beginning of the blizzard to make sure they didn't go bad with the fridge not staying cold enough. Thankfully my father had thought far enough ahead to put some of the lunch meat on the front porch over night so that it froze and brought it inside around lunchtime for it to thaw enough to eat. It wasn't great, but this would be the last meal we would eat the lunch meat.

Before we settled down to play the games, we all grabbed plates of food to occupy us while we gamed. I checked the game schedule and saw that my break wasn't until the last round, so I brought my food with me to the Chinese Checkers table where I would start my game.

The first round of gaming started and I played a mean game of Chinese Checkers against Anna, Clark, and Dave. I was winning for most of it but I ended up falling behind and I came in third place which was disappointing, but I guess it was better than last place. At least I got a point up on the board.

The loser at our table had been Anna and at first I felt terrible that not only had she lost her husband, but also the game of Chinese Checkers. But then I realized that she seemed to be happy just playing the game and chatting with all of us as she did it.

It was funny, though, that as soon as we started this game competition, the entire mood of the house changed. Before it had felt like we were all descending slowly into madness. But even though the storm still raged outside, the mood inside had lightened considerably. The living room was once again filled with sounds of laughter and fun. And if I could continue to push the murder out of my mind, I think I'd be just fine riding out the rest of the storm here.

•Chapter Thirty•

For the next two hours, we rotated through the next two rounds of gaming. I played and completely lost a trivia game, but I managed to win my game of Snakes and Ladders. With a total of six points, I was solidly in the middle of the leader board going into the fourth round.

By that time, I had moved on from cheese and crackers to cookies and hot chocolate. The nice, hot mug of hot chocolate warmed my hands nicely as I sipped up the sweet drink. I had, of course, first overloaded it with marshmallows that I had eaten with a spoon as soon as they were halfway melty before I moved on to the semi-boring, but still wanted hot chocolate.

Looking around the room as we waited for the last game of the third round to finish up. The trivia game was taking an awfully long time as there was a very heated tie for first between Joe and my father, so I sat and observed while sipping my drink.

Considering all of the tension earlier, things were quite pleasant now at the B&B. Everyone looked happy, especially Anna. She was sitting at the Snakes and Ladders table with the biggest smile she had worn since before Jake died, having just won second place.

Even was having fun. Right now she was chatting and laughing with Mandy on the couch as they munched on crackers and discussed the different games that had just ended. I knew that if my mother's idea was good enough to keep my siblings and I at bay when we were younger, it was enough to keep happy too.

The fourth round was my last round to play and this time I was playing Crazy Eights with my father, Dawn, and Claudia. I swallowed the last dregs of my hot chocolate and went about shuffling the cards for the game. Claudia joined me and I gave her half of the deck to shuffle. We laughed together at the competition so far. Just like me, Claudia was stuck at the middle of the pack but she didn't seem to mind.

Dawn was standing by the leader board, staring at the numbers intently. She was towards the top of the leader board and I assumed she was figuring out what was the worst she could do to still win the entire competition. Really, she could lose one of her games and still have a chance to win.

Suddenly, a cheer went up at the trivia table and I turned to see my father triumphantly pumping his arms in the air with a giant smile on his face. I couldn't help but feel proud of him. My father hadn't gone to college, but he was smart as a whip. Whenever he was able to showcase his intelligence, I couldn't help but feel proud of him.

Claudia and I swapped some cards and shuffled them a little bit more as my mother wrote the new points total up on the board. My father was at the top of the leader board along with Joe. The last two rounds were anyone's game, though, so it would be interesting to see how it would play out.

My mother started a five minute timer so that people could take a bathroom break and refill their snack plates before we started the fourth round of gaming. I stood up and decided I could use a few more pieces of cheese and some crackers.

Looking around, I almost couldn't believe that there was a point in time where we were at each other's throats. Right now, everyone was laughing and smiling as they snacked. It made me happy to know that even when we are all stuck together in a blizzard and one of us killed someone, we could still put that aside and have fun together.

The timer dinged and we all started to drift to the next round. I went back to the Crazy Eights table where the cards were already shuffled and waiting for us. My father picked them up and dealt them out to start the game. My starting hand was not great. I had already lost all hope of winning this competition, so I didn't really mind.

The game progressed and my father was absolutely trouncing us. I may have been a little biased, but I was cheering him on to win the entire thing. It was funny though because my father was so humble. He was actually apologetic every time he won or made a move that put him ahead of someone else.

Claudia was in a good mood and I realized that I had grown to like her. Even though I was a bit skeptical of her choice of spouse, she was really pleasant. I was surprised that Claudia was actually quite a bit younger than I thought. Simply because of the fact that she was married to Lyle, who was nearing retirement age, I had assumed that Claudia was about the same age. But sitting next to her as we played a game, I realized that she was actually much nearer to my age. I wondered how someone as young and lovely as her had ended up with grumpy Lyle.

Dawn, on the other hand, seemed incredibly distracted. She kept staring off into space over my shoulder and we would have to remind her that it was her turn. It was like she kept snapping in and out of reality. I wondered what was the problem. Was it the money problems she had mentioned before? Or maybe Jake's death was weighing heavily on her mind. I wasn't going to ask her about it.

As we went through the game, I played a valiant game, but ended up losing which gave me zero points to add to my already sad total. I really didn't mind because we had a great time playing. I had always been someone who was more about playing the game than winning. Most of my siblings were incredibly competitive and while I did enjoy winning every once in a while, I was not one to flip the board when I was losing or gloat when I was the one who won.

We were the first game done during this round, followed closely by Chinese Checkers. My mother scurried over from the Chinese Checkers game to the poster board so she could record the points from each game. Claudia went to report our standings and as it became apparent that there was no way I would be anywhere near the top of the leader board, I was just excited to see that my father was in first place. The last round was also his break, but Joe would be playing and could tie it up for first place.

After all of the points were recorded, it looked like the most exciting thing would be figuring out who would come out in first place. The race for third wasn't as tight, but Joe and my father were neck in neck. We didn't really have a plan for what to do if they were tied after all five rounds were done. I wandered over to the leader board, trying to think up a plan of what to do.

"I think your father might win it all," my mother whispered conspiratorially. Her eyes were shining with love and pride for my father, and I couldn't help but smile along with her. Their love story was one of my favorites because now even after raising six kids, they still were totally and completely in love with each other.

"He might, but Joe might tie it up in the next round," I said. "I was just trying to figure out what we should do if they do end up tied. We can't just leave it that way, not after spending the entire afternoon organizing this competition."

My mother nodded, but before we could say anything, Dawn walked up. Her hair was still in a french braid, but she hadn't bothered to re-do it this morning, so there were wisps of hair flying all over the place. Her eyes were sparkling with a thought.

"Don't worry," she said as she pointed at me. "I have a great idea."

I glanced at my mother, but she had moved on to the food table. She was looking up and down to see what needed to be refilled to make the people happy. Owning a B&B really did suit her because she was definitely the hostess with the mostess.

"Okay," I said. "Tell me more."

I was hoping she had some kind of fantastical, wonderful, out of the ordinary idea that would really cap off this experience on a good note. Hopefully the storm would die down now and we could end this strange couple of days with the end of the games competition.

•Chapter Thirty-One•

"I think that obviously your father and Joe will need to play another game together to figure out who the ultimate, overall winner is," Dawn said. Her eyes were glittering with possibilities, but there was something else behind it that I couldn't read.

Honestly, I had been hoping for something a little bit more exciting. Obviously we were going to have them play another game to break the possible tie. I was a little annoyed that Dawn was acting like she had just come up with a wonderful, new idea that we never would have thought of.

"Well yes," I said. "I think it's quite obvious that we will need to figure out another game for them to break the tie, if they end up tied of course."

Dawn's eyes lit up as she stuck her pointer finger in the air. Her face erupted with happiness, a smile spreading across her face. There was something disconcerting about her smile though, and I found myself a little taken aback by it.

"When we were down in the basement, I

saw a backgammon set," she said. "That would be the perfect, two-person game to settle the tie. Would you go downstairs with me to get it? I don't think I'm supposed to go down there by myself."

I went back and forth in my mind. I really didn't want to go back down into the dark basement, but someone would have to. I suppose that was actually a good idea for a game to break the tie.

"Okay, that would work," I said. "Let me just tell someone else."

I looked around for someone to tell the plan to, but Dawn grabbed my arm a bit too forcefully and whirled me around to face her.

"No no," she said. "You don't have to tell anyone. I mean, everyone is busy watching the last round. We will be really fast and when we come back up, we will tell them the plan."

Dawn was right. Everyone was watching the last round intently, especially the Chinese Checkers game where Joe was trying his best to come in first. It wouldn't take that long to get the backgammon set, so we could just tell everyone the plan once we came back with the game.

I grabbed my flashlight and pushed

through the door to the kitchen with Dawn following close behind me. I hated going down to the basement, but this time should take even less time than when we had to get the tables and chairs plus I was one of the only ones who knew where the backgammon set could be. My mother and father were still overseeing the game competition and honestly, I wanted Tank to stay with Lyle because even if he wasn't my number one suspect anymore, he still had an anger problem that could flare up anytime.

When I got to the door to the basement, I opened the door and stood at the top of the stairs for a few minutes. Staring down into that dark void, even with a beam of light from my flashlight, was daunting. It felt like a deep hole just waiting to swallow me up.

"What's wrong?" Dawn asked. "Let's go."

"I just..." I started, not really wanting to tell a stranger that I was scared of the dark. It sounded so childish even if it was true. "I just really don't like the basement and how dark it is."

"Oh, well we have flashlights," Dawn said with a smile, waving the flashlight in her hand.

I nodded and turned back to the steps.

Gingerly, I started to walk down them with one hand on the railing and the other gripping my flashlight. I shone the beam of light on the stairs, not wanting to miss a step. The last thing we needed was for me to tumble down these stairs and get hurt.

I took a few steps down the old, linoleum covered stairs. As always, they creaked underneath me but in a house as old as this, everything creaked. Once I was about halfway down, I realized that I hadn't heard Dawn start down yet. I turned and saw her waiting at the top of the steps, looking down at me with a wild look in her eyes.

"Come on," I said. "You have to tell me about where you saw it. I won't be able to find it in the dark, otherwise."

Dawn stood still for a moment, staring at me as if she were deciding whether to follow me down or not. I made a decision that I was not going to look around down here by myself. Just as I put my foot on the stair above me to start climbing back up, Dawn started to come down the stairs.

Satisfied that she was going to accompany me down, I turned around and started back down the stairs. As I wondered what her problem was, the already dark stairs became noticeably darker. I turned just in time to see Dawn closing the door behind her.

"What are you doing?" I said, my voice sounding a bit more desperate than I wanted to. "Open the door. It's too dark down here."

"Well the basement is cold," Dawn said, her voice sounding casual. I could almost hear her shrug. "I didn't want the draft to come up and make the living room and kitchen even colder than they already are."

"Okay," I said slowly. "Let's just go fast."

I walked down the last few steps down to the concrete floor and I could hear Dawn's footsteps coming down behind me. The basement seemed so much darker than it had just a few hours ago when we had come down to fetch tables and chairs. Of course, it was just the same. I wondered if maybe I should have asked Mandy to come down with us. Maybe she had helped last time.

Slowly, I spun around, using my flashlight to do a quick search of the shelves that lined the basement walls. I didn't see the backgammon set right off the bat.

"Show me where you saw the backgammon board," I said as I started my second circle around with the beam of light.

"Oh, I think it was somewhere back here," Dawn said. "Follow me over here."

Dawn brushed past me and started walking towards the second room of the basement. I couldn't remember having been back there when we came down for the tables, but I had been more focused on getting in and out as fast as possible, so Dawn could have taken a little look round while I was busy trying not to panic.

Thinking about panic made me realize that panic was slowly setting in again. I focused on swallowing it down and taking deep breaths as I followed Dawn into the next room, further into the bowels of the basement, where it seemed to be even darker. I was starting to regret agreeing to come down here again.

•Chapter Thirty-Two•

As I walked into the second room of the basement, it felt like it was so dark that I couldn't see my hand in front of my face. Whereas before the darkness was surrounding me, now the darkness seemed to be pressing in. It seemed to be taking on a life of it's own and it seemed to be some kind of bully.

My breath started to become more staggered as I exhaled. I could feel what people termed as "impending doom" coming up my throat along with the feeling of stomach acid. It was almost like I had acid reflux except I knew it was just sheer panic.

I hated this feeling and I especially hated that there was nothing I could really do about it. Short of leaving the dark basement or making the power come back on, this feeling of panic would settle itself deep down inside of me until I was able to leave the darkness behind.

"Come on Tessa," Dawn said. "It's just right over here."

Dawn was holding the flashlight towards me and it was blinding me, but once my eyes got used to it, I could see Dawn's face above the beam of light. It was twisted with some sort of an evil smile, as if she were enjoying watching me start to panic. I couldn't tell if that was true or if I was just interpreting it that way because I was in the beginning stages of a panic attack.

I slowly walked across the small concrete room toward Dawn. As I got closer, she pointed her flashlights towards the wall in front of her and the shelves that ran along it. I squinted as I tried to follow her beam of light, still not seeing the backgammon set.

"Where is it Dawn?" I asked, "I still don't see it."

Dawn took a step towards me and grabbed the flashlight out of my hands. It was so unexpected that by the time I realized what she was doing, she was already holding my flashlight in her other hand. By the time I tried to close my grip on my flashlight, it was already gone.

"Give that back," I squealed, flailing a bit towards Dawn. "What are you doing?"

"I will give it back in a minute," she said. "I just thought you needed more light so you could see where the backgammon set was."

A lightheaded feeling was setting in, so I

tried to start taking deep breaths. I took another step towards Dawn with my hand out, reaching desperately for the flashlight. It felt like the darkness was pressing in even more, setting in even though my eyes were open. I kept trying to open my eyes to see more, but they were already open.

"I'll find the set," I said. I was trying to keep my voice calm, but the more I tried, the more desperate it sounded. "Just give me my flashlight back."

Dawn's face was mostly in shadow which gave her smile an evil sort of look. It gave me a sick feeling in the pit of my stomach as I watched her. Every time I took a step towards her, she took a step back. It was like she was enjoying this little interaction between us. I suddenly fully understood the idea of the game of cat and mouse. She was the powerful cat, leading me as a scared mouse right into her trap.

"You're scared of the dark, aren't you?" she said, her voice coming out in a snide whisper. "You're like a little child. You were like a little child in your bedroom also. When I went to find you there, you were terrified."

"What do you mean?" I asked. "When you were in my bedroom I wasn't scared at all."

Dawn rolled her eyes and sighed loudly. She was annoyed that I wasn't following her line of thought, but I was actually more afraid that I was following exactly what she was saying and I didn't like it.

"I told myself that when you disappeared, I just wanted to talk to you a little bit," Dawn said. "I went through the door into the family section upstairs and figured out where your bedroom was."

As she spoke, Dawn started to walk towards me. She had reeled me into her trap and now she was closing in. The closer she got to me and the more she spoke, the more confidence seemed to fill her up. It was almost like she was swelling up confidence.

"But by the time I got to your room, I realized that absolutely no one else was around," she said. "I knew that you were starting to suspect me, so I was going to use that chance to keep you quiet. I had planned such a wonderful crime and I couldn't let you ruin it by figuring me out."

Her words swirled around me and I stood still for a moment, all fear of the dark being pushed down while I let what Dawn was saying really set in. She had been the one in the hallway when I had fallen asleep in my room. She was the one who killed Jake.

"Look at your face," Dawn said with a cruel laugh. "You had no idea. Here I thought you were so smart and that you had me totally figured out. That is why I tried so hard to get you to look at Lyle and Anna. I threw everything I had at you to make you look at anyone but me. And it worked."

"If it worked, why are you telling me all of this?" I asked. "I have to give you credit, you really did make me looking very seriously at Lyle and especially Anna. I hadn't even thought of you as a suspect for a while. But now you are confessing to me and I'm unsure of why you are doing that."

Dawn took a few more steps towards me. I backed away until my back was right up against the shelf that ran along the wall. I had nowhere to go. The cat had indeed trapped the mouse.

"I am telling you this because I wanted you to know why I have to do this," Dawn said. She was so close now that I could see a sort of madness dancing in her eyes. "This is the perfect opportunity for me. You are the only one smart enough to to put all of the pieces together. And here we are, just the two of us. Don't worry, I'll make sure it looks like an accident."

My breath caught in my throat as Dawn was so close to me that I could feel her breath on my face. I was certain that if there were more light down here, that her eyes would be colored red from all of the vitriol inside of her.

"The more you fight, the harder it will be for both of us," Dawn said.

Suddenly one of the flashlights swung out of the darkness towards me. As the hard metal flashlight connected with the side of my head, fear started to rush in, competing for space with the panic. Pain radiated out from where the flashlight hit just above my ear.

The darkness that surrounded me was suddenly filled with sparkles and I couldn't think about anything except how much my head hurt. I needed to get out of the basement before she could do anything else. If I could make it upstairs, I could get some help. I needed to get out of the basement.

Dawn raised her arm up above her head, but as she tried to bring the flashlight down onto my head, I dodged to the left. As she tried to follow me, I hurriedly faked her out and went around her to the right. Her momentum kept her going left as I was able to get by her and run back to the first room and towards the stairs leading up to the kitchen.

I reached the stairs and started to climb up, trying not to let the panic set in. My adrenaline was pumping and it was filling up the space that had been filled with panic. If I started to panic now, I might not be able to make it up the stairs.

Dawn's footsteps were coming towards me, thumping on the concrete floor. I started up the stairs, knowing that when I made it to the top, I needed to get the police here now. It was bad enough that I had let Dawn slip right by me as a suspect, but I felt even stupider when I realized that I don't think my family owns a backgammon set.

•Chapter Thirty-Three•

My previous fear of the basement stairs had nothing to do with the stairs themselves, but with what could be at the bottom of them. Right now, at the bottom of the stairs was a crazed woman trying to hurt me so I guess I was right about that.

But now when I was trying to climb them in a hurry, I was realizing just how treacherous they really were. They were wood stairs that had been covered at some point in time with linoleum tiles. There were spaces between the steps that seemed to want to swallow my feet up.

I had to go slow, concentrating on every step that I was taking. Every time I tried to go faster, the pain in my head multiplied. The pain was shooting through my head and it felt like my vision was closing in like a box. I tried my hardest to focus on the steps to make sure that I didn't miss a step.

"Oh come on Tessa," Dawn said. Her steps were slow and sure on the concrete. She was full of so much confidence that she wasn't even trying to speed up to get me. "Don't make me chase you. That will just make things so much worse for both of us."

I grabbed the handrail, trying to ignore the pain in my head as I started to climb the stairs. As much as I wanted to rush up the stairs to the door, I knew that I needed to go slow so that I didn't trip. It took effort to make every single step and to make sure I got my foot onto the step instead of slipping off of them.

The pounding in my head was intensifying, becoming so overpowering that I just wanted to lay down and shut my eyes. I could feel the pain spreading throughout my entire body. It was getting hard to focus on anything except the pain.

The twin flashlight beams came through the doorway into the first room. Dawn's face was twisted with a strange sort of glee as she slowly made her way to the stairs. I tried to focus on going up the stairs.

"Tessa, just come back down here," Dawn said. "You are making it so much harder on yourself."

"Are you insane?" I managed to yell. I hoped that maybe someone would happen to be in the kitchen and hear me, but the chances were slim.

"On the contrary," Dawn said. "I think I'm actually quite intelligent. I didn't sign the divorce papers so that our divorce wouldn't be final. I made the perfect plan to kill Jake without suspicion so that I would get the money. And then once you became suspicious, I threw you off the scent by scattering clues around and made you suspect not one, but two different people. And finally, I even managed to lure you down here with some stupid idea of a backgammon set. Just admit it, Tessa. I win."

I should have kept going up the stairs, but I just couldn't help it. I whirled around to face Dawn, which was a mistake. Spinning round so fast made my head pound terribly. By now, Dawn was at the bottom of the steps and I was about halfway up. I just had to have my say. While I always knew that my mouth was my downfall, I didn't know that it meant that literally this time.

"You think this is a game?" I shrieked. I couldn't help it. Now I was just mad. I was so mad that I actually took a step down towards Dawn instead of up towards freedom. "This isn't something you can win, Dawn. You killed a person, a person you used to be in love with. And for what? For money. That is disgusting. You didn't win anything."

Dawn's face was stony as she took a step up towards me. I knew I was in trouble because she was close enough to touch me now. I put all of my effort into making it up the staircase.

I whirled around and started climbing the stairs as fast as I could, one hand holding onto the wooden railing for dear life while the other one tracked along the wall. There was nothing for me to hold with the other hand, but I used the wall to try and keep myself upright.

The pain in my head was excruciating. Blackness was starting to close in and I was having a hard time seeing the stairs in front of me. I just kept putting one foot in front of the other, feeling for the next step and trying not to pass out from the pain.

"Poor Tessa," Dawn said. "She's about to have a nasty fall down the stairs. Good thing I'm here to get some help for her."

I ignored her as I took another step up. I was only about three steps from the door into the kitchen, but this time the step wasn't just another wooden step. This time there was something on the step, something that was making it slippery.

As I stepped up, my foot started sliding around. I had been trying to go as fast as I could, so I had stupidly stepped up before making sure I had my foot solidly on the stair. I tried to hold onto the railing as tightly as I could, flailing my other foot forward to try to find the next step, but it was too late.

I could feel myself falling down the stairs, back down into the darkness of the basement. I tumbled head over feet, hitting step after step until I landed with a hard thud on the concrete floor at the bottom. I could feel bruises starting to pop up instantly all over my body. My eyes were squeezed shut from the pain that was now coursing through my body. My head hurt the most, but every part of my body now felt bruised and battered.

I opened my eyes to see Dawn standing over me. To my surprise, there were tears rolling down her cheeks as she shakily pointed the flashlight beams towards the floor next to my head.

"It wasn't supposed to be like this," she said. "Why did you have to try and figure it out? I thought that if I put fish sauce in his food, that everyone would just think there was some sort of awful accident and no one would ever think twice. I even broke into their room and hid Jake's bag with his medicine to make sure we couldn't get to him in time. You know, I still loved him. Even though he treated me like garbage, a part of me still loved him."

"You don't have to do this, Dawn," I whispered. "You can stop right now and I can help you try to make things right."

"Of course you would say that," Dawn said. Her face twisted back into the sinister sneer she had been wearing before. "You just know that I've won. I've bested you and you want me to quit before I've actually finished everything. Well I can't do that. I need everything to go according to the plan so that I can get that money and pay off my debts."

She still hadn't figured it out. I guess I would have to be the one to break it to her. I took a deep breath before I spoke again.

"It doesn't work that way," I said. "I checked. It only takes one person to sign the divorce papers. Jake signed, so you were legally divorced and he legally married Anna. You are out of luck."

The last thing I remembered before everything went black was Dawn raising the flashlight above her head before smashing it down on the top of my head just as the door to the kitchen opened and all of the power came back on in the B&B.

•Chapter Thirty-Four•

When I came to, I was laying on the couch in the living room. The fire was still crackling in the fireplace, but now a few of the lamps around the room were also on. I could hear the furnace was on and chugging along, trying hard to warm up the house that hadn't been warm for days.

I glanced out the window and saw that while it was still snowing, I could actually see outside. The blizzard must have died down, even if it was still snowing. I wondered briefly if the blizzard was actually over or if this was just another small break in the storm.

"How are you feeling?" came a familiar voice from next to me.

Max was sitting next to the couch, on his knees on the ground. I turned to look at him. His dark eyes were full of worry and concern.

I wanted to ask him what he was doing here, but as I tried to sit up, my head felt like someone was smashing it with a hammer. Suddenly, the memory of Dawn hitting me on the head with a flashlight came rushing back with the pain.

"Where is Dawn," I said, scrambling to try to get off of the couch. I needed to find Dawn and make sure she didn't get away or try to hurt someone else.

But my head was full of so much pain that I ended up falling onto my knees next to the couch. My head was pounding so hard that I could hear the whoosh of my blood flowing in my ears. The light suddenly felt very bright and I squeezed my eyes shut tight. My body felt like it was covered with bruises, but the pain of the bruising paled in comparison to the pain in my head.

"Whoa there, Sweet Thing," Max said softly. He gently picked me up from under my armpits and helped to slide me back up onto the couch. As I put my head back on the pillow, he picked up my feet and put them back on the couch, sitting down next to them.

"Everything is alright," Max said. "Dawn is in custody. Jake's body has been taken to the hospital. The blizzard is winding down. And you are safe because I found you just in time."

"Okay, and just so you know, there is one more clue but I'm not sure how it all fits in," I said. "I found Jake's wedding ring upstairs and I hid it in my room. I should bring you up there and show you."

"Not right now," Max said. "I'll go up and get it in a minute, right now I just need you to sit here and wait for the ambulance."

So many questions were floating around in my head, but every time I tried to grab hold of one, it eluded me. I was having trouble focusing on anything besides the pain in my head, but I finally managed to put a few words together.

"How did you know?" I asked. I tried to focus on his face, but the light was too much and I shut my eyes again.

Max took my hand in his. His hands were large and soft. I'd held his hand so many times that it was familiar and I feel like I could pick his hand out of a lineup. When we held hands, our fingers fit together just so. It wasn't like the times when you tried to hold hands with someone and it ends up feeling a bit awkward. It was never that way with Max.

In fact, everything with Max was familiar. The beautiful thing about our relationship was that it was effortless. We could sit together on the sofa for hours, each doing our own thing but never feel uncomfortable. In that moment in time, holding Max's hand, I wondered why I ever wanted a relationship that was new or different from what Max and I had.

"I could just tell that you were walking yourself straight into trouble," Max said, giving my hand a squeeze. "I knew I had to get to you to make sure you were safe. I don't know what I would do if I lost you."

I had to open my eyes; I had to see Max's face. Slowly, I opened my eyelids, letting the light in a little bit at a time. Once they were fully open, Max's handsome face came fully into view. He gave me a big smile as his eyes searched my face.

"There's my girl," he said quietly.

He gently put his large hand on my cheek and used his thumb to brush away a few tears that were starting to fall. I wasn't sure why I was crying, but I think it was just from the relief of it all. I didn't realize just how much stress was building up inside during the last few days. The murder, the blizzard, Clark, everything together had been taking up all of the spaces in my brain. But now, I could let it all out.

"But how did you know that I was in trouble?" I asked. I pressed him for more because usually I was the one finding more clues and putting them all together. This time, Max had managed to read between the lines and he was the one who put some of the pieces together to figure out I was in trouble.

"I'm not sure, exactly," Max said. "But when you asked me about the divorce and Dawn not signing the papers, it was like it all came into focus. There was just something about Dawn and the fact that she was convinced that she would get his estate just because she didn't actually sign the papers."

"But when I went downstairs, the blizzard was still raging on," I said. "You said your car was stuck at the end of your driveway. How did you get here?"

Max blushed a little bit and looked away. I followed his eyes out the window where I could actually see more than a foot out the window. Sitting next to the cars in the driveway was a white and gold snowmobile that looked like it was older than I was.

"I kind of borrowed the Golden Ghost from my neighbor," Max said.

I snorted with laughter. The pain shooting through my head made me immediately regret that, but I just couldn't help myself.

"The snowmobile has a name?" I said. "It

looks like it is older than either of us."

"Probably because it is," Max said with a laugh. "My elderly neighbor Earl said he bought the Golden Ghost brand new in the early 70's. When I went to ask him about it, he wasn't even sure it would start. But I knew I had to get here so by gum, I got it to start."

"And then you drove it all the way here," I said.

"Yes, I did," Max said. "I bundled up, threw on a snowmobile helmet and drove here as fast as I could safely go. I got here just in time too."

The door from the kitchen opened and Mandy backed into view, spinning to reveal a tray with coffee, water, and some snacks. Of course there were no cookies, but Mandy had put together a delicious, healthy snack tray of vegetables and hummus.

"Could I take the story from here?" Mandy asked as she set the tray on the coffee table. "Because I would love to tell you just the next little bit."

"Be my guest," Max said as a smile played at his lips. He knew what was coming and I wondered what in the world had happened.

"Well, the last round of the board game competition was just wrapping up," Mandy said. "Joe was winning which meant that he and your father were tied for first place. And you know how hard it was to see outside. The snow was swirling everywhere. All of sudden, the front door flew open and in walks someone totally covered by a large snowsuit and a giant helmet."

Mandy started giggling as she tried to continue the story, but every time she tried to talk, a giggle came out. I looked to Max to continue the story, but he started to giggle too. I looked back and forth between them, feeling a bit left out and hoping one of them would recover from the sillies soon. Finally, Mandy took a few deep breaths and continued on with the story.

"Honestly, most of us thought it was the killer, finally making his next appearance to kill us all," Mandy said. The smile on her face was an odd contrast to the story she was telling. "It was pandemonium in here. Most of us were screaming, your mother started throwing pieces from the board games at the killer, and thankfully Tank was all the way across the room because he started charging towards the killer and would have tackled him to the ground if Max hadn't taken off the helmet to reveal that it was him."

I couldn't help but laugh, even if laughing hurt my head. I wished I could have been up here to see it especially because that would have meant not being stuck in the basement with a killer.

"Once I got my helmet off, I could see you weren't here," Max said. "When they said they thought you and Dawn had gone to get a game out of the basement a while ago, I knew you were in big trouble. I opened the door to the basement just as Dawn knocked you out."

For a moment, we all sat in silence, totally aware that if Max had been just a few minutes later, things could have ended up much worse. It was bad enough already; I could hardly move without pain shooting throughout my body. But I was so grateful that Max had followed his gut to come and check on me.

Mandy quietly stood up and walked back into the kitchen. She could sense that we wanted to be alone. Max squeezed my hand again and I looked into his eyes. He was my knight in shining armor.

Max leaned forward and kissed me on the lips. It was a gentle, sweet kiss and I could feel Max's concern and love washing over me. As he pulled back, I opened my eyes and gazed at him. I felt such deep love for him in that moment that I never wanted to be apart from him again.

Out of the corner of my eye, I could see movement from the kitchen door. I looked over, expecting to see Mandy peeking in at us since she always seemed to spy on us. Instead, I saw Clark's shocked face.

At first, I felt bad. But then the memory of Clark kissing came rushing back into my mind. If anything, we were even now. But as the kitchen door softly closed, I pushed Clark out of my mind and focused solely on Max in front of me.

•Chapter Thirty-Five•

Usually my Valentine's Day plans would involve going out for dinner and maybe a movie or some dancing. This year, I was lucky enough to move to the couch in the family room where Max and I were curled up watching a movie. We were watching some dumb comedy and eating pizza, so it didn't even really feel like Valentine's Day.

But then I looked at Max sitting beside me. He was laughing at the dumb movie and every once in a while, he would look at me, to make sure I was comfortable and laughing along. Even though I didn't actually think the movie was that funny, I loved how concerned he was that I enjoyed myself as much as he was.

Mandy had stopped by to check on me before she went out for a fancy dinner with Trevor. Of course she had been wearing a little black dress that looked fabulous on her slim body, even if it was a bit skimpy for the Minnesota winter weather.

It made me a little jealous as Mandy described the eight course menu she and Trevor would be enjoying tonight along with a wine pairing for each course. I was especially jealous because at the hospital I had been told to avoid alcohol for a few weeks and while I'm not a big drinker anyways, it is always hard to be told you can't have something.

I thought back to the hospital. Shortly after I had woken up, the ambulance had arrived to take me to the hospital. Max had been allowed to ride in the back with me. He held my hand the entire way to the hospital, gently stroking the back of my hand with his thumb.

Once in the emergency room, I was given the very obvious news that I had a concussion and my body was pretty bruised up, but overall I was in pretty good shape, all things considered. I tried not to think about all of the ways my encounter of Dawn could have gone worse and instead I focused on how grateful I was that I didn't have any broken bones and I would be released from the hospital right away.

Ever since being released, I had been able to take it easy at home. I had been able to catch up on my true crime podcasts and watch a lot of true crime documentaries because apparently being involved in a real, true crime wasn't enough for me. On the other hand, I'd also read a lot of trashy magazines, rewatched a few seasons of an old sitcom that I loved, and tried to do some number puzzles, but too much thinking hurt my head. Needless to say, I was starting to go a little crazy being cooped up, but I also couldn't do much else without a raging headache and feeling every single bruise the basement stairs had inflicted on my poor body.

But then Max came over on Valentine's night with a hot, cheesy pizza from Mike's, a funny movie, and even a card that was both sweet and corny. It was perfect and I wondered if we could just do this for the rest of our lives. As the credits started to roll, I suddenly realized I hadn't even asked about what had been happening with the case in the last few days. Basically, since I got out of the hospital.

"Hey Max," I said, squeezing his hand. "What happened to Dawn? Did you find out any new information?"

"Once we got her in the interrogation room, she told us everything," Max said.

"Did she mention anything about Jake's wedding ring?" I asked. "That was the one thing that really didn't make any sense to me."

"Yeah, she said that when she took the

cocktail ring, she also took his wedding ring," Max said. "That was more of a vengeance thing than anything else. She was mad as a wet hen that her plan didn't work, even though I'm not sure how she could be so delusional to think it would."

"What exactly was her plan?" I asked.

"Well, she didn't sign the divorce papers because she was under some strange assumption that they would stay secretly married," Max said, rolling his eyes. "She thought she had really pulled the wool over everyone's eyes. Anyway, I think her original plan was to scare Jake enough to run back to her once she told him that their marriage wasn't over. But then when she confronted him during his honeymoon, Jake totally blew her off. Once she knew that he wasn't going to come back to her or give her more money, she expanded her plan to include murder."

I burst into laughter because by the end of his explanation, Max had put on a voice like he was introducing a new true crime podcast series. He knew I had a weakness for them and I knew he was poking fun at me, but I couldn't help but think it was a little funny.

"Okay, I am getting a good picture of her

motive, but how did she actually do all of it?" I asked. "How did the bottle of fish sauce get into Lyle's room?"

"This is where it gets kind of interesting," Max said. "Dawn is from California, so she had no idea that a winter storm could last so long. She figured it would end in a few hours and by the next morning, she could slip out and quietly fly back home while you all thought it was an accident. So when she realized that the storm was going to last for a while, she started to see that she needed to throw off suspicion, which she actually did quite well."

"That's for sure," I said. "I mean, she was on my suspect list, but Anna or Lyle made much more sense and Dawn knew to throw just a little bit of suspicion. It was just enough to make me take a second look without making me suspicious of her."

"Anyways, she sort of barged into Lyle's room one morning under the pretense that she wanted to see what his room looked like," Max said. "As she was pretending to enjoy the view out of his window, she shoved the fish sauce bottle behind the pillow on the couch. And apparently she is pretty good at picking locks, so she picked the lock to the honeymoon suite and hid the bag of medicine while everyone else was downstairs. Then while she was helping bring the dinner plates out, she added a little of the fish sauce and made sure to put it at Lyle's place for dinner."

"It's like she didn't really think through things, but they all just fell into place," I said.

"She was lucky that you didn't catch on," Max said. "But she was also unlucky because you are a great investigator. Of course you would catch on at some point."

I snorted and the pain shot through my head. I squinched my eyes shut and covered them with my hand. Max handed me a glass of water and I took a drink.

"Sorry, but I was definitely not a great investigator during this entire situation," I said. "I was tired and grumpy and I even gave up at the end."

Max took my hands in his and waited until I looked into his dark, friendly eyes. His gaze radiated such love and affection that I would gladly stare into them for hours.

"Tessa, you are a great investigator," Max said. "Everyone has some off days, but you still were the one on the ground, figuring out the clues and trying to put the pieces together despite being stuck in a blizzard with a killer. I don't blame you for taking a break from it."

Tears sprung to my eyes and I wasn't even sure why. I felt a surge of emotion crash over me, dulling the pain just enough to make crying bearable. I loved this man. I wasn't really sure where I stood with Clark and right now, I didn't care.

What I did care about was Max. We had agreed to be together under the condition that we were just having fun. No serious relationship and no monogamy needed because we were just keeping it light and fun. We both had a hard year and didn't want any sort of serious, rebound relationship.

But this felt different. I wasn't really sure what to call it, but I wanted more than what we currently had together. I wanted to be exclusive. I thought back to the 'I love yous' we had exchanged earlier, wondering if we would ever talk about them again.

"Tessa, I don't ever want to see you cry again," Max said, using his thick thumb to wipe away the tears on my cheeks. "I love you. And you don't have to say it back to me, but I want you to know that I love you and I want to be Max and Tessa again, like we used to be."

I started to cry harder; I couldn't help myself. But these were happy tears. Max and I were back together. I would deal with Clark and all of the fallout from this later. For now, I just wanted to be happy and revel in this moment.

"I love you too, Max," I said.

Max leaned forward and gently kissed me on the lips. He tried to sit back, but I put my hand behind his head, my fingers entangled in his blond, curly hair, pulling him back towards me to kiss longer. Max didn't like to show public displays of affection and recently, he didn't want to force affection on a girl with a concussion. But I didn't care. We weren't in public and my concussion would be there whether we stopped kissing or not.

Finally, I let him pull away from me, but not too far. I felt like I had been waiting so long to be together like this. I felt like the world was spinning, but this time it wasn't caused by my concussion.

As Max grabbed the remote and flipped to a different channel to find something, anything to watch that would mean we could cuddle together for longer, I realized that Clark and I had never really talked about what had happened. I mean, we had the one fight after I caught him kissing . But I had no idea where we stood or how I was going to tell him about Max and I being together again.

Right now that didn't matter. As Max started laughing along with the laugh track of an old sitcom, I ran my fingers through his hair and thought about how lucky I was that being stuck in a bed and breakfast during a blizzard with a killer had led me back to the love of my life.

•About the Author•

Linnea West lives in Minnesota with her husband and two children. She taught herself to read at the age of four and published her first poem in a local newspaper at the age of seven. After a turn as a writer for her high school newspaper, she went to school for English Education and Elementary Education. She didn't start writing fiction until she was a full time working mother. Besides reading and writing, she spends her time chasing after her children, watching movies with her husband, and doing puzzle books. Learn more about her and her upcoming books by visiting her website and signing up for her newsletter at linneawestbooks.com.

Note From the Author: Reviews are gold to authors! If you've enjoyed this book, would you consider rating it and reviewing it on Amazon? Thank you!

●Other Books in the Series●

Small Town Minnesota Cozy Mystery Series

Book One-Halloween Hayride Murder
Book Two-Christmas Shop Murder
Book Three-Winter Festival Murder

Made in the USA
Monee, IL
20 February 2022

91517804R10163